Naming Maya

Naming Maya

✤

UMA KRISHNASWAMI

Farrar Straus Giroux / New York

Distributed in Canada by Douglas & McIntyre Ltd.
Printed in the United States of America
Designed by Nancy Goldenberg
First edition, 2004

10 9 8 7 6 5 4 3 2 1

www.fsgkidsbooks.com

Library of Congress Cataloging-in-Publication Data
Krishnaswami, Uma, 1956–
    Naming Maya / Uma Krishnaswami.
        p. cm.
    Summary: When Maya accompanies her mother to India to sell her
grandfather's house, she uncovers family history relating to her parents'
divorce and learns more about herself and her relationship with her
mother.
    ISBN 0-374-35485-5
    [1. Mothers and daughters—Fiction.   2. Divorce—Fiction.
3. Family problems—Fiction.   4. Family life—Fiction.   5. East Indian
Americans—Fiction.   6. Madras (India)—Fiction.   7. India—Fiction.]
I. Title.

PZ7.K8978Nam 2004
[Fic]—dc21

2003048511

To Rosemary

Acknowledgments

I'd like to thank Priya Nair, for raising the questions that led me to Maya's story; my mother, Vasantha Krishnaswami, for showing me the streets, hospitals, police stations, cybercafés, and tea stalls of Mylapore; Sumant and Nikhil, who allowed these characters to move in with us indefinitely; my agent, David Hale Smith, for staying power; Audrey Couloumbis, Elisa Carbone, Jeanne Whitehouse, Katherine Hauth, Lucy Hampson, Rukhsana Khan, Stephanie Farrow, Vaunda Nelson, and my almost-namesake, artist Uma Krishnaswamy, for reviewing drafts raw enough to pucker the reading muscles; Dr. Harold Schiffman, for his help with the glossary; Lisa Rowe Fraustino, for giving me the chance to use the short story form as an incubator for some elements of this novel; and, above all, Janine O'Malley, for helping this book come to be.

Contents

Naming Maya

Mami

❖ The day after Mom and I arrive in India from New Jersey, I watch the number 45B bus screech down the road. It clatters to a halt outside my grandfather's old house that we have come here to sell. Passengers tumble out. Another few feet and the bus will have gone crashing into the tea-and-soda stall that sits at a tilt against the tree on the corner. A narrow escape. The traffic hurries on.

Someone squeaks our front gate open. I look out the window again, and I see a tiny figure with gray hair pulled into a little braid so tight the end of it curls up and sticks out at a defiant angle. I grin to myself, and throw the door open for Kamala Mami.

She pretends to be all formal. "I hear you need a

cook," she says. And then she's whooping with delight to see me, grabbing my face in hands as hard and rough as a coconut shell. She taps her hands against the sides of my head and kisses her fingertips, *smack-smack! "Ayyo,"* she cries. *"Kutti kunju yenna periya rajakumari ayittal!"* Me? A baby bird who has grown into a princess? "Yes, yes!" she insists. She is quick and restless. She does not ask, "Do you remember me?" She assumes—and she is right—that I cannot possibly have forgotten her.

"So, Prema?" she says to my mother. "Why are you so thin? Don't they feed you properly there, in America? Good thing I'm here to cook for you."

I know well from my last visit two years before, right after my grandfather died, that Mami is just a cook the way the monsoon is just a little drizzle.

We missed my grandfather's funeral, because in the Hindu tradition you cremate dead people very soon after they die. Mom says it's probably because Hinduism is a religion born in a hot place, and the heat doesn't allow anyone the luxury of waiting till relatives arrive from far away. My mom's cousin Lakshmi and her husband took care of everything till we got here, and then we all observed thirteen long days of ceremonies. Priests invoked the blessings of the ancestors, and we kept an oil lamp lit to guide my grandfather's soul to its new life. During this time relatives I had never heard of arrived to stay and mourn, and gossip. And eat. Mami kept us kids happy with an endless stream of delicious food. Dad didn't come and Mom couldn't forgive him for that.

Now it seems only minutes before Mami takes possession of the kitchen. She scrubs the floor and pours buckets of water everywhere, and looks like she's been doing it forever. She's also moving pretty fast for someone who appears to be about a hundred years old.

"I don't know about this," says my mother under her breath. But there is no time for discussion. Mom stares at Mami, who is now sloshing at a small flood with a broom that is nothing more than a skinny bunch of reeds tied together.

"Come, come," Mami says to us. "Come and talk to me."

Mom says, "Mami, it's such a surprise to see you! I have to ask, how did you know we were here?"

Mami pauses in her mopping. She says simply, "Lakshmi told me."

Mom looks thoughtful. Mami adds, "I go to see her every now and then. For old times. And to help out when she needs me."

Mom murmurs, "It's good of you, Mami, but we can manage. You shouldn't go to all this trouble."

"Nonsense," says Mami. "I've come to help." *And you can't stop me,* says her chin. "And to see this old house again," she adds.

"I have to sell it."

"You have rented it out for the past two years," says Mami.

"Yes, and look how much trouble that's been for Lakshmi," says Mom. "I'm so far away. She's had to come running every time there's been a problem. Anyway, after the last tenants left, no one else wants to rent it. It's too old and too big."

"It's your house." Mami shrugs.

"Yes," says Mom. Suddenly, the tension between them is as brittle and dry as the broken branches of the old lime tree outside the window.

"It isn't my place to give you advice," says Kamala Mami, "but what would be so wrong with coming back here? To live. What have you got in America now?"

"Mami, we've been through all that. My life is there now. There's no question of coming back." Their talk is a blend of honey and chili powder fighting for room on the tongue.

"All right," says Mami, jutting a bony chin in my direction. "All right, then what about this one? You should think about her."

"Er . . . I think I'll go out in the garden," I say. I snatch up my camera and escape.

Among the tangled bushes and weedy flower beds outside, I make little piles of rocks and think about my parents. The anger feels familiar. It has simmered so long it has become a friend. I knock the rocks over and lay them end to end in a long line that bends and curves about like a river. I get my camera ready to take photos of my river of rocks.

There is a picture I hold inside me, as close as I hold my resentment. It is a picture of us, back when *us* meant "three." Mom and Dad, and me. The timer on the camera has triggered flash, image, and smiles, all in one quick click. My parents' heads are turned toward each other, but they're looking at me. I'm holding both their hands tightly, like a magnet gripping steel. On my face is an openmouthed, gap-toothed six-year-old laugh.

That was before Mom packed up and left our house in New Jersey, and took me with her. Before she and Dad sold the house. Before Dad moved to Texas, to a new job and what he said was a glittering hi-tech future.

The father in that picture has planted himself in my head. He talks to me often. Sometimes it's practically a conversation. It's been happening ever since he went away to Texas and didn't come back. Oh, he came back for the divorce settlement. Then he went away again. I kept thinking that at some point he'd come back for me, but he didn't. At first he called often, and his parents, my grandparents, called too. The calls upset my mother. Over time, they became less frequent.

Here in this wild garden, I step back and take a look through the lens at my river of rocks. My camera feels comfortable, like an extension of my hand. The silver brand name on it is still bright, but the smaller red and white letters on the left-hand side are faded from use. Only the slashing red *X* of the model name, Radical X, remains. My stomach feels tight as I look at the rocks, and the years of sadness in my family come washing over me.

A mother and daughter should be a team. It isn't that way with us. We don't understand each other. Sometimes I think Mom wishes she could have had a different kind of daughter. She doesn't exactly say so, but I can tell by the way she looks at me that I make her nervous. When I was younger I used to wish I had some magic spell that could change things in my family. Fix them. Make them simpler. The Dad voice in my head says, *A mom and a dad should be a team too, right?*

My oldest memory is of climbing on the arm of a great wide sofa in our house in New Jersey, and gripping the soft fabric with my fingers and toes. I was standing on tiptoe to look up at a framed print that hung on the wall above the couch. It was a scene from the Ramayana. In it the prince Rama and his beautiful wife, Sita, have been exiled to the forest by Rama's jealous stepmother. A row of smooth round rocks curves about like a river, winding through the grounds. Rama's heart is so good and Sita's is so gentle that all the animals of the forest gather around them in peace. Lions and deer, tigers and sheep and peacocks, play and rest together in that picture. "See," they say to Rama and Sita, "while you are here, we can't fight with one another."

Dad came up behind me, and lifted me high so I could look right at the print. The red and yellow and black shapes in the picture blurred into pure color as I got closer. I didn't have to turn around to know Mom was there too. I could hear her laughing.

But I am not a strong enough glue to hold them together. Looking at the river of rocks I have made in this warm, bright garden, I know that what I want, more than anything, is for that image of my family to be whole again.

Picture This

It takes Kamala Mami only one more day to put the house in order, and then she announces she needs to go shopping. Mom, she says, has bought barely enough to feed a couple of birds. How would two eggplants and a handful of rice possibly be enough for a growing child like me? Mom counts out rupee notes for her, and gives her a list. Mami promptly tucks the money away, and says she knows exactly what to get, not to worry.

She winks at me. She is a swift mover, this Mami. I am not used to her style. The adults in my life have generally belonged to one of two categories: slow and deliberate or quick and angry. I have always been quick and unthinking. I was always the clumsy kid who ran first and thought later.

Quick and deliberate is new to me.

Mom seems relieved when I tell her I'll go shopping with Mami. She's probably been wondering what to do with me while she goes about the business of selling Thatha's house. She has pulled her hair back into a ponytail for the heat, only to have wisps of it escape about her head like smoke, black tinged with gray. She looks beautiful and distant. She stuffs papers into an old brown briefcase, getting ready to go out.

"Where are you going?" I ask.

"To the real estate office. I have to sign a contract."

I follow her out to the street to call an auto rickshaw. The little cabs cobbled onto small motorbike engines are everywhere, their drivers scouting the sidewalks for possible customers.

One of the cabs pulls up alongside, and waits expectantly, his engine sputtering. "Luz Church Road," says my mother. He nods, and they bargain briefly over the fare.

"Mom," I say, "why doesn't Mami want you to sell the house?"

She purses her lips as she gets into the rickshaw, as if she's looking for words that have gotten mislaid. "Mami and I go back a long way," she says at last. "She doesn't understand that this is something I have to do."

Gas fumes plume out of the auto rickshaw exhaust.

The revving engine drowns out her goodbye. Dust scatters, and my mother is gone.

I am not sure how much help Kamala Mami actually needs. But I go to the kitchen and tell her I'm ready whenever she is. "Wait two minutes," she says, and I wait, tugging at my cotton *salwar kameez*. Its long tunic feels dressy over loose cuffed pants. I've grumbled about this, but Mom has paid me no mind. "This is India" is all she'll say when I complain. "You just can't go around in shorts, and that's that."

Mami tidies up, gives the kitchen counter a final swipe. She tucks into her mouth a roll of the betel leaf she likes to chew. It causes her to interrupt conversations in order to dash outside and shoot a dark red stream of juice into a handy flower bed or drain. Now she gathers up an armload of shopping bags, from faded burlap sacks to a plastic affair with handles. I get my camera, and we set out.

Mami walks at a brisk clip. I do my best to keep up. On and off the sidewalk we go, weaving through pedestrians, cyclists, occasional cars, and auto rickshaws. Here and there we detour to avoid a cow, or a couple of goats. And I stop to take pictures.

We pass a huge tree, its umbrella of leaves reaching halfway across the road. "Just a minute," I tell Mami.

"I have to get this one." The tree is so big its trunk has chewed into a low brick wall, splitting it in two right at the corner. In the alcove formed by the split, someone has placed a little statue of Ganesha. People walking by have left flowers and coins in this roadside shrine to the plump, cheery elephant-headed god. With a nod and a *namaskaram*, palms joined, to Ganesha (or Vinayagar, Ganapathi, Pillaiyyar—pick any one of his 108 names!), Mami settles on her haunches to wait for me, right there on the sidewalk. She chews comfortably on her betel leaf. I begin to click.

I am working my way down from the tree's feathery leaves, along its massive trunk, and to the top of the wall, when a stick goes clunk on the pavement, so close to my feet I jump. I look up into a pair of stern eyes in a mustachioed face. A policeman in a crisp khaki uniform stands before me like a pillar.

"*Ey, paapa,*" says a voice like stone. "No photos."

I've done something wrong.

Mami swoops to my rescue. She stands as tall as her four feet ten inches will allow, and meets the policeman's eyes unflinching. "She's from foreign places," she says to him. "She's never seen a tree like this before."

The policeman isn't budging. "This is a police station, do you know that?" He jerks a hand, palm up, toward a sign. It reads, in large red Tamil and English letters, MYLAPORE TRAFFIC POLICE SUBSTATION, NO. 2 A.

Mami shifts into high gear. "I know how to read," she tells him. "And I also know there are thugs and bandits breaking the law all over this city, and you are here, harassing a small child." She pauses for effect, and raises her voice a notch, bringing a couple of cops out from the station to see what's going on.

"*Kali-yugam,*" says Mami. "It's the age of sinners, when a child can't take a picture of a tree. This tree, where Pillaiyyar himself has chosen to live in its shade." She knocks her fists on the side of her head, a gesture to Ganesha, the thing you do when you visit his shrine at the temple. Even I know that. The Hindu Association Culture Camp was big on Ganesha. All the summers I attended, we read stories about him and made the sweet dumplings, *modakas*, that he's supposed to like. But in New Jersey, Ganesha can't be found on street corners.

Mami sets her chin at mustachio-face. His move next. He backs off, mumbling something about police security.

"Yes, yes," says Mami, "everyone can see how dangerous is my Maya." She turns and spits a stream of red betel juice expertly, so that it arcs over my foot and lands in the gutter. It's all I can do not to jump again.

We proceed on our way. Mami is triumphant. I am a little shaky from all this excitement. "What did I do?" I ask her. "I didn't know I wasn't supposed to take pictures there."

"*Tchah!* You did nothing wrong. When real problems are too big to solve," says Mami, "some people make up little ones, just so they can feel better." She grins at me, and I feel suddenly protected.

We finish our shopping. I am damp with sweat by the time we get home. A woman stands next door on the porch of the Rama Rao house. She bangs on the door, and then she yells across to us, "*Ey akka,* you know where these people went?"

Akka, thangachi, mama, mami. Total strangers call each other big sister, little sister, uncle, auntie, as if they're the closest of relatives.

Mami yells back over the wall, "What do I know, sister?"

The woman grumbles, packing a betel leaf into her mouth and chewing it deliberately as she gives up on the door and strolls over to the wall. "*Ayyo,*" she says, "they're a pain to work for. Make you scrub the floor five times over, and the coffee's terrible!"

"Enough," warns Mami. "Watch your tongue."

"Okay, okay, so she tells me to go, it's all right. But

I want my pay. You got an extra two rupees? Bus fare?"

Mami slips her a folded two-rupee note. "All right," she says. "Off with you." A final grumble and the woman makes a run for the bus.

The bird calls are so loud they beat into my brain. "That bird," Mami says, pointing up into a tree where something unseen is shouting out its song, "is called the brain-fever bird." I can understand why. This heat and brightness and bustle would be enough to give anyone's brain a fever.

Spelling Things Out

❖ Mom's cousin Lakshmi comes by the following evening with her kids, a girl about my age and a little boy. The girl's name is Sumati. Last time I was here, we combed each other's hair and giggled together.

Every time I come to India it's like entering another world, a world that gets on fine without me in between my visits. Not only that, but they keep changing all the names. This city used to be Madras. Now it's called Chennai. Thatha's house used to be number 237. Now it's 216. It's one big puzzle, only I can't tell how all the pieces fit together.

Sumati had become a friend when I was here after Thatha died. When I went back to New Jersey, we traded postcards for a few months, and then lost touch, just from getting busy with everyday things.

Sumati gets out of the car and struggles to open the gate for the car while her mom and kid brother stay inside. She's grown taller. She wears glasses now. Her hair hangs in a long ponytail, down to her waist. Her flip-flops are worn at the heels. Auntie taps her hands impatiently on the steering wheel. The little brother makes faces at me.

From next door, Mr. Balaji Rama Rao (retired stamp vendor, Tamil Nadu High Court) waves his newspaper and shouts, "Good evening. No rain as yet! Southwest monsoon is a flop this year, what?"

Mr. Rama Rao is a neighborhood landmark. He is like the mango tree on the corner. He often spends his days on the porch calling out weather reports to any-one who cares to listen. Who needs radio or TV? It's possible to keep up with rainfall and drought patterns by tuning in to Mr. Rama Rao. "Hot and humid again, I see." "Cloudy day—good sign!" One way or another, everybody—coming and going, people and goats and stray yellow dogs—everybody knows him. Mom comes out to greet her cousin and has to endure the weather report as well, while I run over to help Sumati with the gate.

Mrs. Rama Rao emerges to talk to the woman who

brings her cow by every evening and milks it in front of their house, squirting frothy warm milk into a tall aluminum pail. Mr. Rama Rao is fussy about the milk for his coffee. He won't take any of "this newfangled homogenized stuff packed into plastic bags."

"Raoji tells me he met Kamala at the bus stop," Mr. Rama Rao's wife calls out to my mother. She always refers to her husband respectfully as Raoji. "I must come and see her soon."

"Yes," Mom shouts back. "Please do." It seems a strange way to carry on a conversation, shouting over a wall. Mom has told me Mami and Mrs. Rama Rao are old friends, from back in the days when Mami worked for my grandfather.

"Nice lady and such a cook," says Mrs. Rama Rao. "I myself have learned many recipes from her. Devoted to your mother she was, *ayyo*, not like this or that de- voted. Took care of her when she was sick and all, when you were just a little *paapa*."

Balaji smiles and nods and waves his paper. "Not a cloud in the sky," he says.

"Terrible trouble finding household help these days," adds his wife. "Everyone wants to go work for this- company-that-company so they can get benefits and holiday pay. Sloppy work, that's all we get. Take that Radha who does our sweeping-mopping. I tell you, I don't know how much longer I can put up with her. Always wanting advance pay, always rushing through her work because she has five other houses. Can't blame her, everyone needs money, but what are we middle-class people to do?"

While Mom is trying to disentangle herself, Lakshmi Auntie fusses about parking the car. She drives carefully and slowly through the gate, stopping a dozen times to ask, "Is that all right? Do I have room on that side?"

"Ouch." Sumati peers at her thumb that the gate has pinched. "It's okay, not a mortal injury. Hi, Maya. You look different." She speaks in quick spurts, with laughter for punctuation. "Remember him?" She nods at her little brother making faces. "Ashwin. Also goes by 'Pest,' 'Nuisance,' 'Hey You' . . . " Sumati is one of those people you can pick up a conversation with where you left off, no matter how long it's been.

Lakshmi Auntie is out of the car now, smoothing crisp sari pleats into place. We go through a series of hugs and exclamations. Auntie smells of vanilla and starched cotton. Her hug is brief and bony—an efficient hug.

Mom herds us all inside, and Lakshmi Auntie spots Mami. "My goodness, if it isn't Kamala Mami! Don't tell me. You took the bus all the way."

Mami has settled into place like a weed taking root. "Ah-uh," she protests. "What's so bad about taking the bus? Don't scold me. You sound like my son." She gets up and gives her a fierce hug. Lakshmi Auntie cannot get off with one of those quick and bony jobs. She has to be enveloped in Mami's embrace. I stifle my laughter at Kamala Mami in action. I have never seen anyone being hugged into submission before.

"Prema, Lakshmi," says Mami happily, beaming at my mother and her cousin. "It's so nice to be with you girls again." And she breaks into song in the grimy old kitchen as she mixes tamarind and water and chops curry leaves. Her pebbly voice grinds and grates its way over the lyrics.

"Eat," she urges. "Stay and eat." Lakshmi Auntie protests mildly ("No need, Mami, it's only trouble for you"). At first I think she means it, but soon I see it is all part of a social dance. Mami insists, and Mom joins her. "Of course. You must." In minutes Mami has produced a platter of crispy plantain chips, dusted with salt and a trace of chili powder. Then she shoos us out of the kitchen so she can make dinner.

While Mom and Lakshmi Auntie go off to get caught up in the living room ("Drawing room," says Sumati, over my protests that we don't draw a thing in there other than curtains to keep the sun out), we kids sprawl on the cool stone dining-room floor, crunching plantain chips and talking.

"How was your trip?" Sumati asks.

"Horrible," I say. "Too much to eat and nothing to do. Lines to stand in. Baggage to check. Arguing with Mom about everything from the window shade to the crossword puzzle."

Sumati grins sympathetically.

"I really didn't even want to come," I tell her.

"Oh?"

"I told Mom she should just let me stay with my friend Joanie. But, 'No, Maya, a month is far too long.' So here I am."

"Joanie? She's your best friend, right?"

"Yeah. I've known her since we were both in kindergarten."

Sumati says, "Well, if you think traveling with your mom is a pain, you should try a holiday with Ashwin." She tells me of a time she went by train from Chennai to Delhi with her parents and Ashwin. By the end of the long trip the bathrooms had become a little—"whiffy," she says. "They were whiffy. The Pest won't go unless the bathrooms are clean. Just wouldn't go, can you believe that?" Ashwin giggles.

"For how long?"

"Twenty-four hours," says Sumati. "Nothing. By the end of it, talk about wriggle. He was jelly. Quivering. Mass of. In the house, and *zzzzip!*"—she zips her hands past each other to show how—"He spent the next hour in the bog."

"The which?"

"Bog. Loo. *Toi*let." And Sumati puts on a crossed-eyes constipated look that has me laughing till my sides hurt.

"*Akka*, shh." Ashwin protests, but he laughs too.

We start a game of hangman. Ashwin insists on going first. "Me against Maya *akka*," he says. He frowns in concentration, and pencils in his first set of blanks.

I pick a letter, and another, and another. I go swiftly to my execution.

"Hangman!" Ashwin announces in triumph. "The word is *boy*."

"You're being too nice," says Sumati. "It's not good to let the Pest win the first round."

Ashwin sticks his tongue out at her, and says to me, "Okay, it's your turn. Sumati *akka* and me against you." He adds generously, "I'll let you beat us, if you like."

I space out the underlines for *airplane*.

"*I*," says Ashwin.

From behind us in the drawing room, murmurs of conversation rise and fall in small tides.

"*N*," says Sumati. "Hello? You there, Maya?"

"What?" I pull myself back to hangman, and put the *n* into its place.

Ashwin purses his lips. "*P*." I fill the *p* in where it belongs.

Mom and Lakshmi Auntie wander years down the road, and their talk grows softer. Phrases like "difficult for you" and "so sad" float out. I strain to listen, but I lose them.

"*A*," says Sumati.

I put the *a*'s in the right spaces.

"That's not a word," Ashwin complains. To my surprise, Sumati agrees.

"It is too." I give up on eavesdropping. "We traveled here on one."

"Hmm. What? Oh!" Sumati throws up her hands in exasperation. "*Airplane*. American spelling. I should have guessed."

"It's *aeroplane*." Ashwin looks at me triumphantly.

"How do you spell it?" I ask him.

"I don't know." He races around the room pretending to be one.

"Aer-*o*-plane," Sumati corrects me. "*A-e-r-o*."

We do some more words. Sumati wins a few rounds

in a row. I get one, *lurch*, almost by accident. When all the other vowels have failed, what else could it be but a *u*?

"What does it mean?" Ashwin asks.

"A movement, right?" I offer. "Kind of jerking or swaying?"

"Yes, and it also means to cheat someone. Or desert them. To leave in the lurch," says Sumati. "To leave someone in an unpleasant or difficult position."

To leave in the lurch. Obviously, I reflect, as Mami rounds all of us up for dinner, I have a lot to learn.

We eat while darkness descends outside. I am starving, which delights Mami greatly. She heaps steaming rice on our plates, and dribbles a few drops of *ghee* onto it. Then she spoons up generous servings of vegetables and spicy sour *sambar*, with crisp fried *appalam* on the side.

We work our way through this feast. Mami refills water glasses and makes small encouraging noises when it seems as if Ashwin's attention is wandering away from his vegetables.

"When do we get to see Kullan?" Mom asks.

"Oh, he just got this *huge* contract in Bangalore, something to do with redesigning traffic flow in the city. He's a total stranger to us these days, I swear. Puts in a guest appearance between trips. Such a nuisance that he has to work *so* hard," says Lakshmi Auntie, looking not a bit put out.

Lakshmi Auntie's husband is named Krishnan, but somehow, despite being almost six feet tall, he has managed to acquire the name of Kullan, "Shorty." The big family joke is that when I first saw him I was frightened and burst out crying because I'd never seen someone that tall before. I just know they will tell this story at every family gathering till I am forty years old.

Auntie goes on to talk about Ashwin's school, Sumati's school, and her job at an ad agency. "Everyone says the economy's down, but clients keep on coming, you wouldn't believe the work. I have to keep such long hours, and I bring copy home to write all the time. Poor kids, both parents in the rat race."

Mom makes sympathetic murmurs.

"Rat race, rat race," sings Ashwin, as he finishes all his rice and makes little hills with his eggplant. He rolls the words about, liking the sound of them. "What's a rat race?" he asks Sumati.

"Hmm?" Sumati is working on a mustard seed that has lodged itself between her teeth. "It's very hard," she points out when I laugh, "to do this gracefully."

"What's a rat race?" demands Ashwin.

Sumati says, "A tough and competitive pressured lifestyle with *no* time left for silly little boys."

Ashwin complains to his mother, "Maya and Sumati are being mean to me."

"That's nice, *raja*." She isn't listening.

"A rat race is when the other rats are mean to you, and you have to run away," I say.

"Where will I go?" he asks.

"Texas," I say, thinking of Dad, and then I catch myself, grateful that Mom is deep in conversation with her cousin, and has not heard.

Sumati gives me a curious look.

Mami is dishing out sweet *sojji halwa*, with its garnish of saffron and cashew nuts. A generous scoop of it hovers over Ashwin's plate, making him wring his hands because the smell of it is so tantalizing.

"Ah!" He digs in. So do we all. The grainy sweetness of its cream of wheat is perfect and full. "You like it?" says Mami. "When I was a child in Trichy, we used to have this every Friday afternoon. But in wartime everything was rationed—*sojji*, sugar, butter, everything—so for more than one year, no *sojji-bajji*. Those English people fought their war, and we had to give up our sugar."

"The Indo-Pak war?" asks Ashwin. The border wars

between India and Pakistan are the only kind he's ever heard of.

"*Illai, kutti,*" says Mami. "Great big war. The Second World War."

"Oh." Ashwin looks a bit baffled, but I think, *Only Mami can produce a meal so good it makes you exclaim out loud, and then use it to bring history alive.*

Mami serves the final round of rice and yogurt ("because ending with a sweet is not good for you"). Then she retires to the kitchen to eat in her preferred way— cross-legged on the floor, with the plate in front of her, her fingers expertly gathering up the rice and vegetables. Tables are only for softies like us.

Our mothers launch into the old days—picnics at places with wild and beautiful names, Gingee Fort and Vedanthangal. They wander up through time, chuckling over friends and relatives, most of whom I do not know. "Did Rajan Mama's son Ajit ever get married?" "How many people?" "Good grief, why spend that much money on a wedding?" "What about his sister Priya?" "Twins—really? Heavens, poor thing." "Is it true that Uttam's daughter Raji is going to architecture school?" "Is Sriram doing well?" "Oh, dear, software company layoffs? It's the way it goes." "Two kids, really cute but *so* spoiled." They laugh out loud, and interrupt each other, talking over each other's sentences in the way that everyone seems to talk in India.

Later, after they're all gone and Mom is upstairs trying to persuade the terrace door to latch properly (Lakshmi Auntie having cautioned her at length about the increase in burglary rates in Chennai), I help Mami clean up in the kitchen.

While we're putting away all the pots and pans, she takes a strand of my hair between her fingers and clucks over it. "Did you put oil in your hair this morning?"

"Oil? What for?"

Mami rolls her eyes at my ignorance. "It'll all fall out if you don't," she warns, and proceeds to give me a talking to on the virtues of rubbing coconut oil into my hair and scalp every morning.

"Ew." I back away from the bottle she produces from somewhere. That makes her laugh so hard she nearly drops it.

"I don't think so," I say as firmly as I can. "I'm not putting that stuff in my hair."

Mami tries to convince me it will give me long, shiny, beautiful black hair. She points out places my hair is turning brown—like some white girl's. *"Vellaikkara ponnu,"* she scoffs. I protest that I am not a white girl, and that I like my hair the way it is.

"Stubborn," says Mami, "like your mother."

I do not think I am like my mother at all. I don't want to be like my mother. I nibble on a hangnail.

"Tchah, yecchal," she scolds, and makes me go wash my hands. "We went to Gingee Fort when your mother was younger than you are now. Shall I tell you?"

She keeps on talking, so I do not have a chance to answer. Perhaps it's the heat, or the clacking rhythms of her voice, but I am pulled into this story.

"Your mother decided we had to go on a picnic. When we got there, the place was overrun with monkeys. Those monkeys, *ayyo!*

" 'Let's go,' your grandfather said. 'Can't we find a better picnic place?' " Her eyes are alight with those old days.

"There we were, four adults—your grandfather, grandmother, the driver, and me. And we're all saying, 'Let's go. Please, enough picnic.' But Prema refused to budge, and of course if Prema insisted a stork had only one leg, Lakshmi would follow her lead. The girls clamored, 'No, no, we have to have our picnic here.' "

"So what happened?"

"We had to get back in the car, because otherwise they'd come and snatch the food out of our hands. So we ate our whole meal in the car, and all the time those monkeys were sitting on top of the car, on the

hood, everywhere, picking lice off one another. Snarl-
ing at us too, and leaping at the glass to try to get at
our food." She laughs at the memory, and says softly,
"That child had your grandfather wrapped around her
finger. In his eyes, she could do no wrong."

Back When

❦ Lakshmi Auntie drops Sumati off with us a couple of days later, and scurries a protesting Ashwin away for a haircut. Mom is pacing up and down in front of the house, waiting for possible buyers who are supposed to come and take a look at it. Twice already, the real estate agent has sent a ragged-looking urchin pedaling frantically on a bicycle all the way down the road from his office to ask, "Are they here yet?" So far there is no sign of these prospective buyers.

The day promises to turn from plain hot to furnace hot. But Sumati has money. "My auntie on my father's side," she explains, "forgets my birthday every single year. Then she feels bad. A letter from her means money!" We count out enough rupee notes from her fat wallet to get ourselves ice-cold lemon sodas from the corner tea-and-soda stall.

"My treat," she says, and glows with the light of being generous.

Sumati and I bring back the bottles, the red letters on them, Limca, already beginning to bead with cold drops. The soda is sweet and lemony-fizzy, perfect for this day that is so humid the air sits on the back of your neck like a wet sponge. We take the sodas upstairs to my room and lie on the bed so we can feel the air from the whirring ceiling fan.

"Summer," she says. "Hot, hotter, hottest. But no school, thank goodness."

I agree.

"I hate school," she says.

I am surprised. She means it.

"Why?"

She makes a face. "I liked my last school. It was nice and I had friends. Then Mummy decided this was a better school, but the kids are *so* snobby. It's been a year already and still no one wants to be friends with poor old me."

"I'll be friends," I say, "with poor old you."

We laugh. "Okay," she says. "So, what would you be doing back home if you weren't here?"

I tell her about the Hindu Association's Culture

Camp. "I don't know if I would've gone this year, but I've been going most summers. It's okay, but we do the same thing every year."

She turns up her nose. She does not think it is a worthwhile way to spend the summer, listening to stories and taking dance lessons. "Oh, well," she says. "All I'm doing is taking music lessons, so I can't talk."

"Music? What kind of music?"

"Carnatic. You know, South Indian classical. I play the flute." She says it sort of soft and shy, as if she's confiding a secret. "Do you play an instrument?"

"Not unless my camera counts."

"Oh, yeah. I think your mom sent us a picture you took once."

"Really? Which one?"

"Years ago. No, wait, you were in it, so you couldn't have taken it. You were—oh, I don't know, maybe six years old?"

That is the year we bought my camera. Only it was Dad's camera then. He got me started on taking pictures with it. When he left it behind, it became mine. I feel myself tensing.

"You're in the middle, in that picture." She stumbles on, realizing she doesn't mean to go there, but now she cannot stop. "Between your parents. Oh, dear, I'm sorry."

"It's all right," I tell her, but I can feel a smile pasting itself automatically on my face.

Mom comes looking for us. She is carrying her purse, and she's armed with an umbrella against the sun's glare. "You're going out?" I ask her. "In this heat?"

"Just to the real estate agent's," she says. "I'll be back soon."

"The buyers didn't come?" I ask her.

She says, "No. They didn't show up."

Mami has made cool side dishes to go with lunch, lots of yogurt and cucumber, and grated carrots with lime juice and a mustard seed garnish. We are not hungry. The heat saps hunger, and all we want is to drink huge quantities of water.

Mami worries about Mom. "She went off without eating," she says. "You should have told her to eat and then go. It's not good for her."

"Why would she listen to me?" I retort. "She hasn't listened to me in years."

"What do you mean?" Sumati wants to know.

I tell her. "She and my dad stopped talking to each other years ago. By the time I was nine years old, they hardly said ten words to each other most days. I guess when you don't talk there's no listening to worry about, so maybe she just got out of the habit."

Sumati looks surprised. "That must have been hard for you," she says.

"They used to get me to do the talking. You know, 'Tell your mother I'm going to the post office.' 'Tell your father dinner's ready.' That kind of thing."

"They were both still listening to you then," she says.

"I guess," I say, "but I was only a messenger. Bad as that was, it was even worse when they did talk. I'd try to find reasons to make them talk to me, especially Dad, so they wouldn't be yelling at each other."

"When did your parents get divorced?" she asks.

"Well, they separated a year ago. A month before my eleventh birthday. Some gift. The divorce was after that."

"Ever see him?" she asks.

"No."

"Miss him?"

I shrug casually, not letting on. "I guess." Because although she makes me laugh, and we can talk about nothing and everything for hours, she is not yet to be trusted. "Not that much."

"It must be hard," she says.

Mami still says nothing, but in passing behind my chair, as we get up from lunch and begin clearing away the plates, she rests her rough hand for a moment on my shoulder, so I can feel its warmth.

Ashwin survives his haircut with a fuzz of hair all across the top of his head and his ears sticking out. Lakshmi Auntie picks up Sumati. She says, "Kullan's coming back from Bangalore tonight. Honestly, I'm starting to feel like a taxi service."

Ashwin complains that his neck itches.

"You can go home and wash off the bits of hair. You could probably use a bath anyway, stinko," says Sumati.

They drive off. Their friendly bickering is just another reminder that these people might be part of our larger family, but their lives are very different from ours.

On the Sidewalk

The trouble in my family began with naming me. Thatha, Mom's father, had my name picked out even before I was born. Two names, actually, because he didn't know I was going to be a girl and he wasn't taking any chances. He also figured that since he was the only grandparent on my mom's side he needed to be doubly prepared. Dad's parents had a girl's name picked out too. The only problem was it wasn't the same name. Mom liked Maya, so Maya I became. Dad didn't care. It would have been fine if it had stopped there, but it didn't. When Thatha called us, and wanted to talk to me, he'd ask for Maya. But when Dad's parents telephoned, they'd ask for Preeta. For a while I answered to both.

At Hindu Culture Camp they told us Maya was the name of the Buddha's mother. I wasn't sure how I felt about that, since she'd died seven days after he was born. And even if she'd lived, her son would have left her to go off and teach the world. Great for the world, but what about poor Queen Maya? Joanie, who always tried to help when I had parent problems, once suggested, "Why don't you just make 'Preeta' your middle name?" But when I asked Mom, she said, "Well, it says 'Maya' on the birth certificate and you don't have a middle name." So I waffled between names, and sometimes I used them like weapons. When I was mad at Mom, I wouldn't answer to "Maya." Once, I annoyed her for days by saying, "Maya's gone away. I'm Preeta."

I asked Dad, "Which name do you like?" and he said, "I like them both. Why don't you use the one *you* like?" Only how was I supposed to choose and still please them both? I grew into Maya from habit, but Preeta still hung out there, a ghost-name waiting in the wings, crying, *Choose me, choose me!*

"You are very quiet," Mami says to me on one of our shopping trips. I have taken to helping her haul the heavy produce from the market. We are eating so many tons of fresh vegetables I am in danger of turning into an okra or an eggplant.

"You have trouble in your heart," she says. "It's difficult for you, because you don't understand."

I protest. "What don't I understand?"

"Things," she says. "Grownup things. Things that should never have happened."

"Like my parents being divorced?" There. I've said it. Why does it sound so terrible? Like something to be ashamed of. I think she's going to tell me to be quiet. That is, after all, the response I have gotten from Mom when I have dared to raise the issue. She usually gets a pained look and says, "Maya, we need to move on. What's the point of feeling bad about things that can't be changed?" To anyone else that would sound like good advice. To me their divorce is a wound that won't close up the way it's supposed to, like an itch from a scab that has not quite healed. How can you leave something behind when it's been hidden so carefully from you that you never even knew what it was until it was too late?

But this is Mami. She is not going to fuss about what's okay and not okay to talk about. She laughs out loud. She says, "People aren't always as they seem to be. Even your mother."

Oh, yes? What is Mami going to tell me now?

"Once when your mother was just a little thing, she decided she was going to run away from home."

"Why?" I asked.

"Well, she was bored one afternoon, and your grandmother had scolded her for something she'd done, or hadn't done. It probably just seemed like a good idea at the time."

I am forced to smile. Who can imagine a mother doing things like that? "Where did she go?"

"Not far. The mango tree. She decided to go live in the tree. She left a note on the dining table saying, 'I am running away. *Don't* look for me in the mango tree.'

"Well, of course your grandmother found the note, and she laughed and laughed. 'Shall I send the gardener up the tree and get her down?' your grandfather asked. 'No,' she said. 'Let the child run away for a while.'

"So we waited, and every time he said, 'Now?' she'd reply, 'No, let her be. Not yet.'

"Well, finally your grandmother let him send the gardener up the tree, and there she was, your mother. She was a bit nervous, because you see it was getting dark, and she knew that mosquitoes start to buzz for people's blood in the evenings. But when your grandfather said, 'Did you have a good time?' she just looked at him, determined as anything, and replied, 'Oh, yes. There are lions and tigers up there! It's wonderful.' "

All around us, the city buzzes. I try to see my mother as a little kid with fancies in her head, and lions and tigers up in the imaginary world of her mango tree. What I cannot understand is why Mami sighs, as if this were a sad, sad story instead of just a funny one. She keeps on walking. She says, "The next time she ran away was to get married."

I know that story. It used to be a romantic and mysterious family tale. That was before it became erased by arguments over everything from money to me. "Your grandfather didn't want them to get married, you know."

I know that too. It seemed no one had wanted them to get married. And if they hadn't, where would I be? I point that out to Mami. She laughs. "You might be the only good thing that came of all this," she says.

I object. "That's not true. It wasn't always bad. They didn't always fight. It just got that way."

"Divorce," says Mami. "No such thing in my day. The woman just stayed and suffered, that's the way it was. Maybe it's better now."

The noise picks up around us. Big black songbirds party in the neem and mango trees that line the roads. *Kuyil*, Mami says they are called. In India, even the birds are loud, all yelling at the same time, so different from the finches in New Jersey that take turns singing civilized little songs. Looking up to see them, and paying more attention to my thoughts than to the world around me, I don't see the crack in the sidewalk ahead. Where my feet expect flat pavement, slabs of concrete have been ripped out for a construction project. I go sprawling. I try to put my hands out to break the fall, but end up in the dirt anyway.

"*Ayyo, ayyo!*" Mami cries, and rushes to help me.

"I'm all right," I say. "I tripped. I'm fine." I get up and dust myself off. I pick up the shopping bags and begin gathering the scattered potatoes and greens. And then all at once, I feel a familiar sticky hot trickle in my nose and watch in dismay as the first warm drop of blood falls on my pale-green cotton *kameez*.

Terrible timing.

When I was younger I used to have frequent nosebleeds. Not the little drippy jobs some kids get. These were gushing fountains that spouted out of my nose and over everything in sight. By the time I'd put ice on my forehead and pinched my nostrils together, and reassured people, "Don't worry. It's okay, I'll be all right," I'd be covered with enough blood, you'd think I was the goddess Durga herself, coming back from battling the buffalo demon Mahisha. No lion for me to ride, though.

My mother is funny about blood, so she'd get really

flustered whenever it happened. Dad would get me to sit up, lean my head back, pinch my nostrils, cool down. Then he'd get me a big glass of juice.

Over the years he was there less and less. Sometimes he'd be around, but too wrapped up in work to help me. He'd say, "Coming, Maya, I'll be there in just a minute," but then I began to figure out that wasn't always true.

He had quit his job and tried to start a business, something to do with the stock market. The basement became an office, where before it had been one big playroom for me.

One weekend when I was eight, Mom was out grocery shopping and the telephone rang. Dad was in the office, which was where he'd begun to spend a lot of time, sometimes even falling asleep at his desk. I picked it up.

"Preeta, is that you? How nicely you answer the phone!" My grandmother asked to speak to Dad.

"Daddy," I called. "It's Ammamma for you."

He picked it up in the basement. I tiptoed to the bottom of the stairs and listened. He kept on clacking those keys and talking on the phone, but soon his voice rose higher, drowning out the frantic *tap-tap-tap* of his fingers on the computer keyboard.

It was then that I felt a tickle in my nostril. I stood in his office, but he didn't even notice me. He was too busy arguing with his mother on the phone. When Mom came home I lied to her. "I had a nosebleed, and Daddy helped me," I said. Because of course I knew that if he could have, he would have.

Ever since then, when it happened, I'd go in the bathroom to take care of it, then I'd wash up and cool off when it was over, and I'd get a drink afterward. And I wouldn't tell my parents about it.

Here on the sidewalk, with a hundred people gathering around to gawk at me, I don't feel so capable.

No problem, as it turns out. Kamala Mami handles the crowds. She swears and fusses ("Fools! *Madaya! Muttal!* Don't you have anything better to do than stand around and cast evil eyes on this poor child?") until they leave us alone. She gets me into a little grocery store crammed with tins of everything from cooking oil to baby powder. Mami makes me sit on the dusty floor and lean back on a sack of rice. She gets the man in the store to turn on a giant electric fan so the cool air swishes on my face. She buys a green coconut from the old man selling them on the sidewalk, and asks him to hack it open for me. Then she sticks a straw in it, and holds it in her cracked old hands while I drain it gratefully.

"Sit still and don't try to talk," Mami warns.

That's fine with me.

She chants the way she does at home, in the

kitchen, or while she's lighting incense sticks in her little shrine. *"Annapurni, sadaapurni . . . "* She chants the names of Devi, the goddess, giver of food and killer of demons. She tells stories of all the forms the goddess can take when she comes down to earth, some sweet and loving, and some strong and fierce.

"The buffalo demon thought he was safe," she says. "He thought no man or god could harm him, and so his pride grew monstrous. And in the end who killed him? Devi! No man or god, do you understand?"

I understand. I sip the clear sweet coconut juice, and I am grateful for Mami, who seems every bit as fierce as any goddess.

"Killed him, just like that," she says with relish, and the shopkeeper warns her, "Shh. Please. My customers."

Mami waves him away and carries on. "Devi, mother of us all, she'll take care of you."

Sometimes Mami talks to the shopkeeper, who is still nearby. He is wearing a strained look by this time, trying to assure concerned customers that everything is fine. And sometimes it seems to me, although I can't be sure of it, that she is talking to no one at all.

Of course Mom goes into a flap when I return home with great splotches of blood all over my *kameez*. "Oh, no, Maya! Are you all right? Oh, my God, look at all that blood."

Exhausted, I lower myself onto the broad wooden seat of the *oonjal*, the swing that hangs at one end of the dining room. It is so big it could hold half a dozen people. Giant chains suspend it from hooks in the ceiling. Mom brings me a glass of water, and the sight of my bloody *kameez* makes her go shuddery.

"You've not had one of those in so long. I'd hoped—"

"Yeah, me too. But it's okay. Mami helped me." Mami is out of help mode now. She tells Mom in detail all about it, and how she's looked after lots of children, and never seen anything like this. Do many children in America have nosebleeds? Maybe it's the food. Or the cold weather, very unhealthy.

Mom tries to answer the questions, but it is a bit like trying to stop one of the city buses by waving at it. And anyway, Mami isn't waiting for answers. She is recapping how she cussed out the people who tried to gather around while I lay bleeding to death on the sidewalk. I can't tell if I am imagining it or if she's really talking too much, too loud, too long. I decide I'm just tired. Finally she runs out of steam and wanders away to get laundry off the clothesline. Mom and I are left alone sharing an awkward silence.

I twiddle the pages of a book lying open on the *oonjal*.

"Maybe you shouldn't have gone out in the heat," says my mother at last.

I really don't think she means anything by it. It is something to say.

But I have had it. The day, the dreadful sticky hot nosebleed, the dust, the dirty sidewalk, Kamala Mami and her ramblings, the crowds of people—it is all too much.

"Oh, sure." My voice comes out sharp and high-pitched, what Joanie calls my "tangry voice," teary and angry. "Blame me. It's my fault! I had the nosebleed because I chose to go out, right? You weren't even there!"

"Maya!" I've stopped her in her tracks. "You know I didn't mean—"

But I swing my legs off the *oonjal*, fling the book to the floor, and march out, noting with terrible triumph that my words have landed smack on target, every single one.

The Cottage
at the Beach

❖ The days get hotter. Mom gets busier. She also gets nervous when I venture anywhere outside the house. We have conversations that go like this:

Me: I'm going to walk up the street and take some photos, okay?

Mom: I'll come with you.

Me: It's all right, I'll be fine. I thought you had to go get those papers notarized.

Mom: Yes. Well, maybe Mami can go with you.

Me: Maybe I'll just go another time.

I don't even go to the store with Mami when we run out of beans and rice because Lakshmi Auntie picks up groceries for us on her way home from work. She insists it's to save Mami the hassle of walking to the shops in the heat, but I think maybe Mom has told her about my nosebleed.

I do make my way up onto the flat terrace roof and get some great shots of the city. One day I surprise a rhesus monkey sitting on the edge of the roof. He sidles up to me. I back away. He stops, scratches himself, and comes closer. I remember Mami saying, "They'd come and snatch the food out of our hands." I retreat, in case he decides to make a grab for my camera. Only later do I think, *Oops, missed a photo op.*

After that I stay indoors and thumb through all the moth-eaten books in the glass-fronted cupboard on the landing. Issues of *The Strand Magazine* with the original Sherlock Holmes stories. Scads of children's books by a writer named Enid Blyton, about little English kids having tea and going to the seaside.

Mrs. Rama Rao comes to chat with Mami. Mami goes next door to sample Mrs. Rama Rao's new mango pickles.

Prospective buyers begin to arrive in small groups. They walk through the house, pointing out flaws as if we are not even there. A few relatives drop by to say hello to Mom. I begin to put some faces to the names I have heard Mom and Auntie mention—Uttam's daughter Raji, and Priya with the twins. They come and go like minor whirlwinds. Predictably they say, "Is this Maya? How she's grown. Is this Maya who cried when she saw Kullan because he was *so* tall?"

Lakshmi Auntie asks about others. "Did Ajit and his wife come to see you? What about . . . ?" She names a few others.

"No," says Mom. "It's okay, Lakshmi. I'm not here to hold court with the family."

But Auntie sniffs and says, "They are so rude."

Mom suggests that perhaps the family does not approve of my parents' divorce. "What is wrong with them?" says Lakshmi Auntie. "How totally medieval. What do they think, it's contagious?"

Lakshmi Auntie invites me to go with Sumati and Ashwin and her to the beach for a couple of days. "Come on," she says. "Your mother's busy. What will you do here by yourself? We'll take a cottage. It'll be a change for you, and you girls can have some time together."

"Yes, do come," says Sumati.

Even Ashwin begs. "The beach! Yes, Maya *akka*, come with us!"

"Go, Maya," says Mom. "Lakshmi's right. It must be getting pretty boring for you here, hanging around the house."

Well, that's true enough. Mom certainly doesn't have time for me. I'm only in the way.

"All right," I say to Sumati, "I'll come."

On the drive to the beach, Lakshmi Auntie chatters like a rattly set of window blinds.

The "cottage" turns out to be a flat-roofed one-room house, painted pink, with a deep covered porch. A hammock dangles outside, slung between two coconut trees. We lug our suitcases inside. The room is painted like the inside of a peach. It has only one bed in it.

"Where do we sleep?" I ask.

Sumati looks around. A rolled-up pile of mattresses and sheets rests across the arms of a wooden chair. "We unroll those and sleep on the floor."

"Like camping," I say.

Ashwin sits on the bed and swings his legs. After a few minutes he says, "I'm bored."

"Come on," says Lakshmi Auntie. "Let's go sit out in the hammock and read a book." She pulls copies of *Chachaji*, a children's magazine, out of a tote bag, and Ashwin follows her out.

"Want to go for a walk?" Sumati asks. "I'll take you to a special place."

"Sure." I check the film in my camera and slip a new roll into my pocket.

Outside, Lakshmi Auntie and Ashwin have settled

down to the riddles page of *Chachaji*. The laziness of sea and sand and sky has even managed to slow Ashwin down.

"Maybe you'll grow up to be a photographer," says Sumati, "like my uncle."

"Your uncle's a photographer?"

"My father's younger brother. He works for a newspaper in Delhi. He travels all over the place."

"What about your dad?"

"What about him?" Sumati is leading the way toward the water, up a steep sand dune covered with some kind of trailing weed. I am barefoot, and the green stems feel like ropes between my toes.

"He travels a lot too, right?"

She wrinkles her nose, considering. "Yeah, he's always gone. But so? We know he'll be back. And then he'll go again, somewhere else, and then come back. It's how it is."

She sounds so sure, it twists my insides.

We reach the top of the dune. Talking while climbing, I haven't paid attention to where we are going. Now I look down, and see how far we've come. The row of pink box cottages stretches away far behind us. Before us is the gray sea, flecked with white foam. The waves reach across the horizon. You can't see where they begin and end.

We sit on the highest point of this high hill of sand. I dig my heels in, and wiggle my behind into place. Waxy weeds tickle the back of my legs where my *salwar* has scrunched up.

"This is my special place," Sumati says. "I can sit here and listen to the ocean for hours."

We listen together. The ocean grumbles like an old woman, pulling its waves back, gathering its voice, then returning steadily to slap the shore. It reminds me of Mami, her voice burbling over the pots and pans in the kitchen. I wonder if she is telling stories today even though I'm not there to listen.

I think of the map at the Hindu Culture Camp, with dot stickers showing where everybody's families came from for three generations. There were yellow dots in different parts of America where most of us kids had been born. There were orange dots for places where parents had been born—many in different parts of India, but some in California and Ohio and New York. A sprinkling of blue dots told of grandparents born in Pakistan and Nepal and Sri Lanka, and even some in America. A few dots were scattered about in Canada; a few more in Guyana and Trinidad, mainly for Dina Ramchurran's family, who were all from there; a few in England and Australia (the Gupta twins and Geeta's uncle Prem); and even one orange dot on the little island of Mauritius out in the Indian Ocean (Coomi's mom, who spoke French and taught us yoga two days a week). All of their faces, and the faces I know in my family, seem to be reflected in this water. Sitting here and looking at the ocean, the world makes sense.

We used to go to the beach in New Jersey, Mom and Dad and I, when I was younger. But all the beaches we went to were white piers and boardwalk and saltwater taffy. Not like this wild place with its single high mountain of sand and this deep gray grumbling ocean. Mom said something about it once. "Isn't it funny how pale everything is here? Even at the beach, all the colors are pastel. In India, everything's so bright." My father disagreed. "Goa has a beach with white sand. White. Can't get paler than white." "That's different," she said, and they stared at the ocean as if they were waiting to see if it would change color.

No muted colors at this beach. Down at the row of cottages, flame-of-the-forest trees hold eye-popping orange flashes of flowers. I look back toward the water. In the distance I can see smudges of fishing boats— one, two, three of them—bobbing around. The air is filled with a sharp sea smell, fish and salt and seaweed. Farther up the beach from where we are, Sumati tells me, the next morning will bring crowds. "See there?

It's where the fishermen take off early, before the sun rises."

I can see the pegs that will hold nets fast to the shore. As she talks I can imagine the women in bright saris tucked up high to keep them out of the water, tying large nets to the pegs.

"One time, when I was five or six," says Sumati, "we came here and I went in the water with my *chappals* on." She points to her flip-flops with the worn-out soles so I'll know what she means.

"I know *chappals*," I tell her. "What do you think I am?"

"Some kind of American, that's what!" she teases.

I shiver.

"What's wrong?" says Sumati.

"It's funny," I say. "I'm American here, but in America, I'm Indian."

"Is that bad?"

"I don't know. Years ago we were going to a friend's house for a party. It was Divali . . ." The Hindu festival of lights was always an occasion to dress up, me in a long silk skirt, with my hair braided and a sticky *bindi* on my forehead.

"And?"

"Oh, it was nothing, really. A bunch of teenagers drove by and shouted at us. They called us dirty dotheads."

Sumati's jaw drops. "That's terrible. That's—why, that's racist!"

"Well, yeah. Of course. But you know, I was only five years old."

"What did you do?"

"I took a really deep breath and gave them the best and biggest raspberry I could manage. I don't know if they saw it, but it made me feel better." She looks puzzled at "raspberry," so I stick out my tongue and show her.

Sumati laughs. "You are something. You know that?"

She pours a trickle of sand onto her feet and watches them disappear. "Go on about your *chappals*," I tell her.

"Oh, it wasn't all that exciting. A big wave came and knocked me over. And when my parents pulled me out, my *chappals* had washed away. I could see them floating off on the water like little boats. My father said they'd go all the way to Singapore, or maybe even Australia."

We laugh about those flip-flops from Sumati's younger, smaller feet, traveling around the world with all its people, some of them with good hearts and some filled with hate. "I cried and cried," she says, and smiles, the way you can smile at your younger self because, after all, what did you know back then? She adds, "They were purple."

I dig my hands into the sand, finding small shells, round ones and little cone-shaped ones, mostly broken, but some whole. There is one little double shell, its two halves still joined at the hinge. It seems too perfect to disturb, so I put it back gently and cover it with sand again.

Sumati slides around till she is lying flat on the ridge of sand. She stretches out and sighs, closing her eyes.

"Say 'pizza,' " I tell her, and get my camera ready.

She opens one eye and makes a funny face. I laugh and click. She sticks out her tongue, and I click again.

"My turn. I'll take your picture. Can I?"

After that we sit for a while, looking at the ocean. From this high up it is like a painting. Soon Ashwin comes yelling for us. "Come see me fly my paper aeroplanes!"

All that evening we help Ashwin flutter his paper planes back and forth across the beach. The next day we walk along the beach and watch a man do his morning yoga. Ashwin tries to stand on his head and the man, distracted, frowns at him.

The day goes by in a warm glow of sunlight on water. We get in the car and drive to a place where ancient temples have been sculpted out of solid rock. The carvings are intricate, each telling a story. A cluster of small temples is strewn on the seashore, each designed to look like a chariot. A larger one, farther away, sends two spires towering up into the sky. "Look," says a man who has appointed himself our guide. "Single rock carved into temples. Seventh century. Pallava dynasty. UNESCO has declared this as a World Heritage Site."

He shows us a panel with an image of the goddess Ganga descending to earth, tumbling down into the great god Shiva's matted locks of hair because if she fell directly the earth couldn't bear the force of her rushing water. Enormous slabs of rock bearing images like this stand scattered among the groups of temples. Unlike the old temples in the city that are still used for worship, these lie deserted. It feels as if something's missing—incense, chants, and people circling the shrines. Ashwin wanders in awe around the massive feet of a carved stone elephant. Next to it he looks tiny.

And then I come face-to-face with a panel that takes my breath away. *"Mahishasuramardhini,"* says our guide proudly. "Goddess Durga defeats evil." The pinkish stone of the giant carved wall gleams in the sunlight. Was it once the wall of yet another temple now in ruins? No one knows. The goddess is slender, almost a girl. One of her many arms pulls back the string of a bow, training the arrow upon her victim. She rides a curly-maned lion. Each of her hands holds part of an armory—knives, clubs, spears, a trident, a whirling discus. A massive demon rises to confront her. His heavy club is raised in readiness. Horns spring from his water-buffalo head.

"Fifty paise for your thoughts," says Sumati.

I shake my head. "That's powerful stuff."

She nods. "Take a picture of it."

I do. The slight stone figure holds me spellbound. Every fold of her robe is delicately sculpted. A tassel dangles from a necklace, swinging away from her graceful body as she aims her arrow. Other figures in the panel shrink back from the two in the middle, making way for the final scene. You know the demon doesn't stand a chance.

"Mami told me this story," I say.

"You're named for a goddess too," says Sumati.

"Me? No, I'm named for Buddha's mother. Can't imagine why."

"Silly," says Sumati patiently, "who do you think Buddha's mother was named for?" Oh. That's a new one. She explains it to slow American me. "One of Devi's names is Mahamaya. *Maha* means great, yeah? Well, she's supposed to have come down to earth and put the army of this wicked king, Kamsa, to sleep.

Then she takes the form of a baby girl, because he's looking for another baby—the infant Krishna. So Kamsa finds her, and then the goddess goes back to her true form." Sumati slams a fist dramatically into the palm of her other hand. "Just like that," she says. "No more Kamsa."

I know about Krishna, of course, from Culture Camp—blue-skinned, naughty Krishna, who was really the god Vishnu, who stole butter from the milkmaids. I'd heard of the wicked king. But I didn't know the goddess played a part. And no one's given me this quick-time version before.

"See?" Sumati smiles. "Maya is not just any old name." She likes it better than her own name. "Sumati is so ordinary," she says.

I tell her about the Great Name War when I was born. How Thatha called me Maya and Dad's parents called me Preeta. "They came to visit us once a year," I say. "Well, until my parents split up. And every single time Dad shouted and Mom cried. But they brought me lots of presents, and we always went out to dinner and the zoo and movies when they came."

"And they called you Preeta? What did you want to be called?"

"I don't know," I say. "Sometimes I liked Preeta. Sometimes I didn't."

"Maybe the name thing wasn't about you at all," Sumati points out. "Maybe it was your mom they didn't like? You know what I mean? So whatever she liked, they'd make sure they liked something else."

I have never thought about it that way before. Sumati goes on, "But that's their problem, right? Not yours. Maybe it's not so bad having two names. That way you get to choose."

What would the goddess say? She has thousands of names, and thousands of forms—some to protect, some to destroy evil, some to change the course of the universe. It strikes me that nothing in India is what it seems to be. Everything has many names, many forms, many meanings. Maybe that's why so much of what I see here is both strangely familiar and just plain strange, all at the same time. Maybe these meanings just show up when you need them. I glance at the goddess. It is surely my imagination, or maybe the shadow of the setting sun, because of course she couldn't possibly have moved her stone lips in a flicker of a smile.

Too soon, it's time to leave. "Madam, come back this evening, please," the tour guide begs Lakshmi Auntie. "Shore temple floodlights will be on. All maintained by Mamallapuram Town Panchayat." Lakshmi Auntie gives him a handful of rupee notes, and he leaves, urging us to return.

A vendor comes by selling hot roasted peanuts in paper cones. Lakshmi Auntie turns up her nose at first, but when Ashwin begs, "Please, Mummy, please, I'm *so* hungry!" she gives in and buys us one each. They are salted, and there is spice in them that creeps up on me, so I eat them without realizing how they will make my eyes water. But maybe it's my own mixed-up feelings that are making that happen. It's hard to tell.

The Movie

❖ When we get back to town I find Mami has cleaned the house till every last doorknob gleams.

She sprinkles water over the front step and the gravel at its foot. Then she pinches some rice flour between her thumb and index finger. Every morning she trickles it out onto the step in fine lines, and then onto the gravel in circles and stars and swirly designs until magical patterns decorate our threshold. By the end of the day they get blown off, swept away, walked over, and then the next day she does it all over again. When I look up and down the road, there are the same kind of kolam patterns on every doorstep, every threshold. But ours are bigger and better because Mami has double the energy that any of those other women have.

"Teach me," I ask her one day after I've taken some pictures. She tries. I am clumsy. She is patient. But as I pour the fine flour into delicate circles and connect-the-dots like hers, my fingers slip and I end up instead with a scattering of flour all over the steps, all over my feet.

And Mami begins to laugh. At first I join her. We laugh together. Then I stop. And she carries on laughing. It is only then that I realize her laughter is too shrill.

She laughs until she has to clutch her stomach and sit down. She laughs and it seems she cannot stop. I am alarmed by the small trickle of saliva that escapes from her mouth, and at the harshness of the laugh as it forces itself out of her throat. Can you die from laughing too hard? Can you be choked by laughter?

She stops suddenly and frowns, as if taken by surprise. She dashes the moistness from the corner of her mouth with the end of her sari, and says to me, unsmiling, "That's enough. I have work to do," as if it is somehow my fault she has nearly died laughing.

I try to decide if there is something here for me to worry about. If Mom were here I could ask her. But she has gone out to get some papers stamped by the notary who sits in a cool dark office under a thatched roof three blocks away. And I decide it is just as well, because what would I ask? Is Mami okay? What reason do I have for thinking she might not be? Laughter is not cause for concern in the world. Is it?

While I am spending time being undecided, Sumati shows up. "Want to go see a movie?" she asks.

"I don't know," I tell her. "Mom's not here."

"Oh, come on. She won't mind, will she?"

"I don't know. She might if she comes home and I'm not here."

"Leave her a note," Sumati suggests. She's so sensible. "No, better. Tell Kamala Mami. She'll tell your mother, no?"

"Hang on," I tell her, and I take a peek at Mami in the kitchen. She is singing to herself as usual. She does not seem as if she's in danger of exploding with laughter. Sumati is behind me, peering over my shoulder.

"Well?" She obviously sees nothing unusual.

"Okay." I'm talked into it.

I tell Mami, "Sumati and I are going to see a movie."

Mami demands at once, "Movie? What movie? Where movie?"

Sumati explains patiently. It's a Tamil movie. Yes, it's okay for kids to see—Mami tells us quite clearly what she thinks of the kind of movie in which the women aren't wearing nearly enough clothes and aren't nearly as good as they ought to be. No, no, it's not one of those. It's close by. We can walk, so we won't have to take the bus. Sumati has enough money for both of us. Yes, she's sure about that. We'll go straight there and back. We won't stop for anything, *sathyam*, Mami. We'll be careful, honest.

"Wait," I say. "Let me go get my camera."

"Why? You're going to see a movie or make one? Oh, all right." Sumati taps her feet impatiently.

I go upstairs and hurry back down with the camera.

"I haven't seen a Tamil movie in years," I say. "We used to rent them from the Indian store in New Jersey, back when."

"They're all the same." She grins and tugs at a coral bead hanging off-center on a chain around her neck. "Long. With songs. Dances. Tears. Ladies with bosoms like a fleet of battleships." She pronounces it "boo-zums," dragging the word out for drama. We giggle, because of course between the two of us we don't have enough boozum for even one battleship.

Mami fusses and carries on. She's worse than Mom. "Just tell my mother," I say to her, "that we'll be back by seven."

She throws us a few more warnings. "Be careful crossing the road." "Count the change they give you." "Come straight back." "Hurry." We are at the gate.

"Don't talk to strangers!" Mami calls out from the front door as we close the gate behind us.

"*Tchah!*" Mr. Balaji Rama Rao flaps his newspaper at us. "Still no rain. And water rationing they are going to implement. Go, go in." This command is not for us. It's aimed at the betel-leaf-chewing woman I've seen at their door before. Last time she was complaining they'd fired her, and now they appear to have hired her back. Mr. Rama Rao seems willing to hold two conversations at once. "Terrible, terrible!" he says to us. "Push the door, I say, it's open," he says to the woman.

We giggle our goodbyes at him. We giggle all the way to the theater. It's a comfortable thing, being silly together. It's the way I am at home with Joanie.

The movie is so stupid it's splendid. It is about four brothers who are identical quadruplets and grow up not knowing anything about one another. "Of course they're identical," Sumati tells me when I finally figure this out. "Quadruplets are always identical." I admire her for being so sure, even though I think she's wrong. There are few things I am that sure about.

There are so many characters in the movie I can't keep them all straight. A karate-kicking grandmother has us in stitches. We love it. We laugh ourselves silly when the entire family is stuck in a house teetering on the hillside with the bad guy coming up to get them.

We laugh so hard and so loud the rest of the audience begins laughing at us, and we don't care a bit. We have such a good time that when the three hours of the movie end and the lights come back on, we sit in our seats blinking, our eyes needing to adjust.

"Oh, that was funny," gasps Sumati.

"That was horrible," I point out to her.

"Horribly funny." We giggle together.

That gets us laughing all over again as we finally emerge from the theater into the still bright and hot evening.

"That grandmother was amazing," I say. "She doesn't get mad. She goes to war!"

"It's an effective strategy," says Sumati. She has such a grand way of talking. Effective. Strategy.

Walking home, we burst out laughing about the movie, again and again. A little boy hawking key rings clowns for us. The tea-stall man shoos a yellow dog away. The mango seller calls out her wares. I take all their pictures so I can cement the day into my memory, seal it in a bubble, and go back to it when I need to smile. It's what pictures do for me.

It's a little past seven by the time I say goodbye to Sumati. I watch her take off toward the corner she will turn to get home. I swing the gate open at the yellow house on St. Mary's Road.

I am completely unprepared for the reception I get when I enter the house.

"Where have you *been*?" Mom's face is as tight as her words. "I've been worried sick about you."

"What—?" It takes a moment before it all registers. "I don't know what you mean. I went to see a movie. With Sumati."

My mother takes a deep breath like she will need it because she has so much to say. "All you needed to do was tell Mami where you were going, and she'd have told me. Honestly, Maya, you're old enough to think of someone other than yourself once in a while. Don't you—"

I say, "But, Mom—"

"I don't want to hear any excuses," she says. "I had a tiring afternoon, and I didn't need to be sitting here since four o'clock, wondering if I should call the police."

Excuses? Fine. If she didn't want my explanation, she wasn't going to hear it. I think of Mami's laughter that won't stop, and I feel a little worry quivering inside me. I am scared this is all part of something I do not understand. A part of me urges, *Tell her, Maya. Speak up. She needs to know.* But another part insists, *You tried to tell her, didn't you? She didn't want to hear a word of it.* The Dad voice says, *Remem-*

ber, there were other things you didn't tell her. Phone calls . . . an overnight letter . . . Yes, better if you don't tell Mom.

Until I get it all sorted out, I have to let my mother's disappointment hang in the air like rain clouds.

Forgetting and Remembering

❖ "Why didn't you tell Amma?" I ask Mami the first moment I get alone with her the following day. "Why didn't you tell her that I went to the movie with Sumati? You said you would."

She is cleaning the dining table. Not that it needs to be any cleaner. You can practically see your face in it now. She pauses in mid-swipe, glancing at me, and then her hand goes back to work.

"Why?" I ask her.

Another look. This one holds secrets, as if she finds something about me funny but isn't about to tell me what. Not yet, anyway.

"I forgot," she says, and begins singing in her usual way, paying no more attention to me than if I'd been one of the crumbs of food she's sweeping up in the cleaning cloth. In between stanzas she mutters, "I forgot. What about it? I forgot." The words are mixed like spurts of laughter into her singing. Her eyes focus on a place somewhere on the wall behind me, so she looks as if she is looking right through me to someone else.

Outside, the crows begin their daily racket.

"How could you, Mami?" I should have the sense to quit, but I am too upset at the unfairness of it. "You didn't tell her, and she got angry at me, and all you can say is you forgot?"

She turns on me a look so strange and scary it makes me take a step back in sudden panic. Her dark eyes are distant. "I forgot," she says with a shrug. "I had other things to remember."

She goes to trim the wick on the lamp she keeps burning all day long. She has set up a small shrine in the alcove in the wall of the dining room. It holds bright pictures of the gods. Mami lights that lamp every morning as soon as she gets off the bus and into the house. She keeps it filled with oil all day so it is still glimmering when she leaves in the evening. By the time she returns the next morning the little flame has died out and she lights it all over again. She recites a long string of Sanskrit verses at the top of her lungs as she does this. Wave upon wave of them roll off her tongue. She begins always with hymns to Devi in her various forms.

The doorbell rings. It is Sumati, waving an American flag. "What are you doing with that?" I ask, letting her in.

"It's the Fourth of July," she says, all excited. "Aren't you supposed to do something? Here, I got the Nuisance to make you a card. He's playing at a friend's house, so I thought I'd come over. I wanted to bake a cake. Don't know how, though, and Amma's gone to work, so I couldn't ask her to help."

I'm so surprised I don't know what to say. The card shows a tall building that looks more like the Eiffel Tower than anything in America. In Ashwin's wobbly handwriting it says, "Happy July Forth." What a lot of trouble they've gone to! "Thanks," I say at last. "Where did you get that flag from?"

"Oh, my photographer uncle brought it back from America for me years ago. I used to collect flags. Here, you want it?"

I dissolve into tears. "What?" she cries in concern. "What did I do? I thought you'd be pleased."

"I—am." I hiccup. "It's just . . . you're so nice. Thank you."

"You always cry when people are nice to you?"

She gives me an awkward little hug. "Stop, silly," she says, which of course makes me even more of a wreck. "Something you need to talk about?"

And that's when my worry about Mami comes out. I tell it poorly, all in a rush, like a bottle of fizzy Limca uncapped too soon after being shaken up.

When I finish, Sumati is silent. "Maybe she just forgot," she suggests at last. "I mean, she's getting old, you know. Old people forget things." She is so filled with cheerful common sense that I feel foolish. Perhaps my imagination is just working overtime. And when Mami comes to see who is here, she seems so much her normal self that Sumati shrugs her shoulders at me as if to say, *See? I told you there's nothing to worry about.*

At first Mami is confused when Sumati tells her it's Independence Day. "No, no," she corrects Sumati. "That is not till August fifteenth. Don't they teach you anything in these schools these days?"

Sumati clarifies. "No, Mami, in America it's Independence Day today."

Mami says, "Oh, why didn't you say so? It's the *vellaikkara* independence!" In celebration of the white people's holiday, she insists on boiling a pot of milk to make *payasam*. She cooks a handful of fine noodles in the milk. She tosses in sugar, and pinches of saffron and cardamom. When she is done, all three of us sit on the *oonjal*. We swing back and forth gently, and sip the hot sweet liquid from little stainless steel cups. Mami wants to know what I would be doing if I were back in America now. She nods enthusiastically when I tell her about fireworks and parades. "People are the same everywhere," she says. "Everyone celebrates special days with fireworks and parades."

After Sumati has said goodbye and gone home, I think, *Lighten up, Maya. Nothing's wrong.*

Mom is Official Mom this afternoon because the real estate agent, Prasad, brings new people to see the house. He takes off his shoes at the door, where people coming into the house are expected to. You can tell who has company in any house up and down the road by the rows of shoes and sandals at the door. He is dressed like one of the billboards that advertise men's clothing, pants ironed to a sharp crease, tie held in place with a little fussy pin.

"How do you like India?" Prasad asks me. He sets his briefcase down and wipes his forehead with a white handkerchief. "You are here in mango season. You like mangoes?"

"Yes," I say. "Yes. I like mangoes."

He and Mom chat about mangoes. They debate politely over the best variety (Alphonso or Banganapalli). On one point Mom agrees with Prasad—you can't get a decent mango in the United States.

The prospective buyers are a husband and wife. They are small and quiet, both of them, matched in size and volume. They talk back and forth to each other, quickly, in undertones, refusing to join in the mango conversation. The wife jots columns of numbers on a floppy notepad and wriggles her toes so her silver toe rings click on the floor.

Mami brings coffee around. It is milky and sweet and steaming hot, with a lovely bitterness that fills the air. I don't like the taste of it much but I love that smell. She looks them all up and down. She urges, "Drink before it gets cold. Best blend of peaberry and robusta." Steam rises from the stainless steel tumblers of coffee, promising they will not cool anytime soon.

"Very good," says Prasad. He takes an obedient sip of the scalding stuff.

"From Narasu's. I ground it myself." Mami beams. I stifle a grin, having been with her on a couple of those coffee-grinding trips. Mami's method is to commandeer the coffee grinder after bullying the owner into admitting he doesn't know the first thing about truly fine coffee. When she's got him to the point where he is begging her to teach him how best to use his own equipment, she then holds up all the other customers till she's got the stuff done to exactly the right consistency. She passes out samples of it to everyone in the store, admires the texture and scent, declares the price outrageous, and only then counts out the rupees.

Prasad finishes his coffee, clears his throat, and says, "Hrmm, shall we?" And Mom says, "Please. Go through the house. I'll be here if you have any questions." Mami takes off reluctantly with the empty tumblers.

Reciting a list of the selling points of the house, Prasad leads the couple into the hallway and up the stairs. "Excellent condition. It has been in the same family for three generations. And of course this is a prime location."

I think perhaps I'll tell Mom about my concerns about Mami, but before I can say anything, she mumbles about going to see if Mami has enough milk money. So I don't get a chance to talk to her. I tell myself that it's all Mom's fault. If she'd wanted to hear me even a little, I'd have shared my worries about Mami with her in the first place. Even if they were needless worries.

That's right, chimes in the Dad voice in my head.

Why didn't she listen to you? Why didn't she tell you there was nothing to worry about?

What did Sumati say when we were playing hangman? To be left in the lurch. I say it to myself a couple of times. In the lurch.

Two-Gift

❖ I am still lurching along and feeling aggrieved the next day, but Mom does not seem to notice. She has other things on her mind. The buyers have decided they are not. Not buyers, that is. Not for this house. "They say it is too old," reports Prasad. "Not enough conveniences. No built-in cupboards, no modern kitchen. Too old and sprawling."

After Prasad has delivered the bad news and gone, my mother sighs and says, "We just have to wait till he finds someone else to see the house. Is there something you'd like to do, Maya? Shall we go look at the shops on Mount Road?"

"I don't care," I say.

"Well, what do you want to do?" Now she asks.

I set my chin. "I don't care," I repeat.

"Does that mean yes or no?" She sounds exasperated.

I shrug. "Yes, I guess." I'll go, but I can't pretend I'm going to enjoy it.

We take an auto rickshaw to Mount Road, which has been renamed something else but everybody still calls it Mount Road. The auto man refuses to make the U-turn it would take to get us to the side of the road we want. He is headed the other way, he says, but we can cross, right here. He points to a little break in the median, and then blasts off with a cheery toot of his horn.

Crossing Mount Road is a little like running an obstacle course in which all the obstacles move with great noise and speed in unpredictable directions. This is because, among other things, drivers don't stop for pedestrians. Some stop for the lone traffic light on the far end of the divided road, but we can't bank on that either. If we want to cross, we have to scope out the oncoming vehicles quickly, then make a mad dash across the road. We keep a swift eye all around so we can dodge cars and buses and motorbikes. They all keep coming. They honk and beep at us for daring to get in their way. We manage to make it safely to the other side, in spite of one blue bus that obviously has us in its sights for target practice.

We end up in a huge dusty cavern of a store filled with carved wooden figures—elephants, camels, birds, masked dolls with spring-mounted heads that dance when you touch them. And little brass bells on strings, and statues sized from tiny to larger than life. I hover around the trays of miniature objects. I've always liked small things. They are comfortable. You can tuck them in your pocket and only you know they're there.

"Want to get something for Joanie?" Mom asks. While I am debating whether to reply, she says, "It's okay, pick something you like. A Two-Gift?"

I stare at her. That's a Dad line.

One gift to keep and one to give away, me to Joanie, Joanie to me. It was a rule we made years ago when we were both much younger. Every time we go anywhere with our families, we bring back two gifts. Looking at our twin collections, you can trace the places we've been the years we've been friends. We each have a replica Capitol (Joanie's visit to Washington, D.C.); a bear bookmark from Arizona (my trip to the Grand Canyon); coral from Florida (Joanie's trip to see her grandma Beth); and Mickey Mouse buttons from Disney World (my sixth-birthday trip).

Dad loved the term *Two-Gift*. Whenever we went anywhere on vacation, he was the one to remind me. "Nothing for Joanie?" he'd ask. "A Two-Gift?"

No Dad to remind me. No Dad to make funny faces, to make me laugh so hard the tears would run down my cheeks and I'd beg for mercy. "Stop, stop. Oh, I'm getting a stick in my side."

Mom would say, "Stitch, sweetheart, stitch." But Dad would pretend he had a stick in his side that wouldn't come loose, and stagger around trying to get it out, and drive us both into a weakness of laughter.

I steal a sideways look at my mother. The only thing that makes her laugh close to that hard these days is chatting with Lakshmi Auntie about old times. Suddenly, despite my determination to stay mad, I want her to laugh with me about something now. But there's no funny memory handy.

From among the baby elephants, I finally pick two. They are carved in a dark wood, each one no bigger than my thumb. Their trunks are raised high. Their ears have a friendly flap to them.

We pay and wait while the cashier wraps the little carvings in great wads of paper and sticks them in a box for us.

Dad, I say to him in my head, *do you like them?* And he answers, *Like them? Of course I like them.*

Thank you, Dad, I say. He doesn't reply so I say it again. *Thank you.*

"You're welcome," says my mother, and I jump. I've spoken out loud without realizing it.

"Hope Joanie likes her elephant," says Mom.

"Huh? Oh, yeah, I hope so too."

We manage to get an auto rickshaw going in the right direction and head for our next stop, the bookstore at the other end of Mount Road. Every once in a while, as the auto rickshaw swerves through traffic or loops around a cow chewing cud in the middle of the road, I can feel Mom looking at me. I stare straight ahead at the smiling movie stars who dance in flimsy neon robes on giant billboards, in between looming ads for cheese and chocolate, cell phones and CD players.

The bookstore turns out to be much more eventful than I have expected. Mom picks up a newspaper and a book for Joanie's mother, *Fabric Arts of India.* Susan is an artist. Her prints and silkscreens sell in galleries and on the Internet.

I pick out some postcards. I think perhaps I will send Joanie one, since, like the Two-Gifts, postcards are a vacation tradition.

We pay, and a doorman ushers us out of Bookmarks, Etc.: The Place for Books and More. "May I see your receipt, madam? Thank you. Please come again." The bookstore is a polite world.

All of a sudden pandemonium erupts on the landing outside. A woman has gotten the hem of her sari caught between two of the metal plates on the down escalator, the ones that mesh together to make a step when the thing rolls you along. She falls heavily, as if falling has made her dense, so that she lands with the crash you'd expect from someone twice her size. The escalator keeps carrying her down, chewing up her sari as it goes. She screams. People scramble, run, jump off, as if the escalator were the sinking *Titanic*.

A little crowd gathers.

The woman shrieks, *"Ayyo, ayyo, yen podavvai, yen podavvai."* Well, we can all see it's her sari, her sari!

People shout instructions to no one, or at least it doesn't look like anyone is listening. "Be still!" "Shut it off!" "Jump off!" "Call security!" And this one: "No panic, please!"

Someone gets the escalator to choke to a halt. The woman yanks herself loose from the folds of her sari, all six yards of its bright pink length. She stands there shaking in her underskirt and blouse, her bright red *pottu* running sweatily down her forehead.

A huddle of people watch as one of the doormen from the bookstore pulls out half-digested bits of pink sari, oil-stained from the escalator's innards. As if the machine is spitting it out because it doesn't taste good.

The woman's face is tight with anger and embarrassment. I stare at her.

A policewoman appears from nowhere, all shiny-bright in stiffly starched khaki pants and tight leather belt and braided hair. She escorts the sariless woman and the rescued remains of her clothing off behind a door marked "Authorized Personnel Only."

We take the stairs down to the street level. Mom waves a passing auto rickshaw to a stop, and we ride home. I wonder what it is like to have an escalator rip your clothes off in public, so you have to pretend dozens of people aren't staring at you.

One Full and One Toned Milk, Please

❖ Sumati shows up the next morning. "Amma sent lime pickles for you," she says, and hands my mother a little jar.

But we are in a crisis. The milk deliveryman hasn't shown up for some reason. Mami is in the kitchen, shaking her head and muttering to herself. There is no milk for coffee, she says, and how can we expect her to cook breakfast until after she's had her coffee? Mom offers her a can of condensed milk. Mami waves it away contemptuously. "Bad enough we have to buy milk in plastic packets from that crook Nazir," she says, "because the wretched milkwoman brings her cow to the Rama Raos' doorstep and milks it for them, but she won't sell any to us. She's just too cheap to feed her cow properly, the poor animal. Did you know her son-in-law tried to kill the cow by feeding it nails? So we have to wait for Nazir to bring us Aavin milk in plastic bags and now even he's disappeared. When I was a girl there was none of this milk in bags. Did you know that they're very bad for your health, you are actually eating bits of plastic that dissolve in the milk? And what about the poor cows out in the street, did you know they are dying from eating plastic bags?"

Mom ducks under this barrage of information that, true or not, is not helping us get any closer to breakfast. Mami wrings her hands and curses the milk deliveryman. She is sure he's taken off with all twenty of the rupees she gave him yesterday. Probably gone all the way to Bangalore by now. Mom tries to reason with Mami—there's no way twenty rupees will get Nazir the milk deliveryman to Bangalore. But she makes no headway.

Sumati says, "No problem, Mami. We'll go get you some milk, Maya and I. What kind do you want?"

Mami switches from despair to joy as quickly as flipping channels on a TV remote. "Full," she says. "No, no, toned. No, one of each. Full is good for coffee, and toned sets better *thayiru.*" I realize she's talking about the milk. Whole is better for coffee. Reduced fat makes better yogurt.

Mom hands us money with a sigh of relief, and we set off.

It's one of those glaringly bright mornings that will soon turn to blistering heat. Mr. Rama Rao is right. There is no sign of rain in this sky.

"Thanks," I say.

Sumati shrugs. "No point in letting her get upset about a thing like milk."

"I know." I fiddle with a button on my *kameez* till it flies off. It lands in the road, and when I step off the sidewalk to retrieve it I am almost knocked over by a passing cyclist. He rides off with an annoyed jangle of his bicycle bell.

"What is the matter with you?" says Sumati. "You're as jumpy as . . . as a mustard seed in a frying pan!"

She makes me grin in spite of myself.

"It's Mami, right?" she says.

I try to whistle and fail miserably. I've never been able to whistle anyway, why would I get it right this time?

She says, "Do you think . . . ?" at the same time as I begin, "That's what I . . ." She stops. "Okay, you go first."

"Mami," I say. "There's something wrong with her."

Sumati says, "She's just upset about the milk. She's touchy about things like that."

"Is that all?"

"I don't know. Amma says she's just getting old."

Our conversation has made the walk seem shorter than it is. The Aavin milk booth is a hole in the wall framed by wooden shutters that are painted a bright blue. It is wedged between a newspaper vendor's stall and the shop where Mami grinds her coffee. The scent of roasting beans fills the air, overpowering the faint nastiness of the rubbish heap on the other side of the road. A cow pushes through early morning traffic to pick a banana peel delicately off the garbage. People cross the road at a quick clip, avoiding the traffic that has already begun to thicken. The cow plods on, her sights set on a clump of flowers hanging over someone's hedge. Overhead, rows of pigeons sit like animated ornaments on the flat roof-edges of apartment buildings.

I am breathing in the day when suddenly I feel Sumati stiffen.

Teenage girls lounge in a gaggle at the bus stop just outside the milk shop. They eye us curiously. I eye them back—tight jeans, tailored jackets, and shoes with platforms so high you'd think only a stilt walker could handle them. Jangly earrings and black lipstick complete the picture. It isn't what you'd see in tourist videos of India.

My mother would go up in a puff of embarrassment

if I dared to dress like that. But, then, I wouldn't dare.

"Oh, no," Sumati mutters.

"What?" I ask. "Do you know them?"

The girls giggle and nudge one another. They concentrate on giving us a collective scornful look.

Sumati doesn't reply at first. I try again.

"Well? Do you?"

She sighs. "Yeah," she whispers. "One of them's in my school, the tall one with the nose ring. She used to live in Paris. She thinks she's so cool."

It is hard to believe these girls share the same town as Sumati, in her rumpled blue *salwar kameez*, let alone the same school.

Joanie was my partner and defender when kids teased me at school. When Mark jeered, "My dad says Maya's dad got fired from his job!" Joanie stuck her tongue out at him and spilled juice on his homework. When he came back with, "My dad says Maya's dad's going to dump her mom!" Joanie ripped into him with fists and nails until Mrs. Harrison pulled them apart and sent them both to the principal's office. But not before Joanie made Mark the Drip (we called him that) say, "Okay, okay, I'll shut up." "Apologize," she insisted. "Apologize to Maya, you little rat."

Now it seems the role of partner and defender is mine.

"Hi, Sumati," says the tall girl, turning her face so her little nose ring glitters. She stretches out the "hi," dragging more sarcasm out of the word than I'd have thought was possible.

"What are you talking to her for?" says one of the others. "*Ayyo*, look at those clothes!"

For the first time since I have met her, Sumati's confidence wavers. The girls giggle at her, secure in numbers. She pulls at her shabby *kameez* as if she is ashamed of it. She is frozen in the spotlight of their attention.

Not me. The look, the tone, the attitude, strike me with a lightning bolt of energy. I know exactly what to do. I feel as I did years ago and far away, when those other teenagers had driven by and yelled insults at us. "Dot-heads!" they'd cried. "Go home, you dirty dot-heads!"

My timing is perfect. I gather energy from inside me. I pause while they consider what to do next. I deliver, with mighty concentration, fueled by all the breath I have in me, a good, large raspberry.

It stops them cold. It's not what they expect. They stare at us in bafflement. There's an uncertain moment when I think, *Oh, boy, I've made it really bad for Sumati now.*

Then the tall girl bursts out laughing, and they all

follow suit. But it's a different kind of laughter now. The tension's broken. They burst into exclamations and questions. "Hey, who's this? Where'd you dig her up from, yeah, Sumati?" It's all good-humored now, take it or leave it.

Sumati introduces me.

"From America, huh? Where?"

"New Jersey," I reply, and feel their surprise at my accent. They can't figure me out. I don't fit their sense of what someone from America should be like.

"So, how come the *desi* clothes?" one of them asks.

I hesitate, wondering why I need to defend my *salwar kameez*. Then, "They fit," I say. "Come on, Sumati."

We walk tall, up the steps to where the Aavin man has been watching with a grin on his face. We say, in one voice, "One full and one toned milk, please."

We walk home with the fat little pillows of milk. We don't speak as we walk. We don't need to. We are a partnership.

Jana

Mom needs to go to the bank the following day, and because Sumati and Ashwin have to go to the tailor and get measured for new school uniforms, and the bank is on the way, we all go together.

The bank is only a few blocks away from the house. Finding parking is such a pain that it seems it might have been easier if we'd walked. "Maybe you should just drop us off, and we'll get back on our own," Mom suggests. Auntie pooh-poohs the idea, insisting, "No trouble at all. Really, Prema, I'm used to driving in this messy place." Between the cows that have taken up grazing stations at the corner trash heap and all the auto rickshaws whose drivers seem to be gathering for an early lunch, it is a stressful matter, but Lakshmi

Auntie manages to wedge us into a tiny space where the car will be out of harm's way.

We sidestep the cows and cross the street, pausing to drop a couple of coins into the bowl of a blind man snapping finger cymbals and singing at the top of his lungs. He has positioned himself strategically just outside the bank, so he can appeal to people going in and out of a place that deals in money.

Under the blue-and-white Union Bank sign, a uniformed guard swings a door open for us. This door is more than an entrance and exit. It is the dividing line between worlds. We leave the bright harsh street behind for a room crowded with dark wooden counters, the only sounds the murmur of conversation, the clacking of computer keys, and the occasional jingling of coins. Overhead the ceiling fans whir to a rhythm of their own. Some things mark this bank so it could be nowhere else in the world but here. At one end of the room, on the wall, there is a large framed poster, offering loans to account holders and listing current interest rates. Above the lettering is a large, friendly Ganesha, beaming at us all. A similar poster hangs on the opposite wall, but the picture on that one is an equally large and friendly Jesus, hand raised in blessing.

My mother asks a teller if she can see the bank manager. "Is Mr. Devadas here today?"

"No, madam. He has gone to Bangalore for his son's wedding. Maybe the assistant manager can help you?"

In no time we are ushered into a back office where a plump woman in a purple sari looks up from her paper-strewn desk and motions to us to sit down. My mother makes her request. She needs to close out a safe-deposit box.

"Certainly. Number? Key? Complete this form, please, and I can help you with that."

My mother begins to fill out the form, when Lakshmi Auntie exclaims, "I know where I've seen you before. You're Jana, right? Kamala Mami's daughter-in-law!"

The woman freezes, then forces a smile. She says, "Yes, and you are . . . ?"

Lakshmi Auntie explains the family connections, how Mami knows three generations of us. She introduces Mom, and then Ashwin, Sumati, and me.

"Did she come to see you?" Jana asks.

There is a brief silence. Then Mom says, "Yes. She insisted she wanted to come and cook for us while we were here. Didn't you know that? At first she wouldn't take any money, but I finally persuaded her that the only way I could let her come every day was if she'd let me pay her."

"We didn't know." Jana shakes her head. "She

doesn't tell us where she's going, what she's doing. My husband is really worried about her. And she lives all alone. She doesn't have to, you know. She's getting old, and she forgets things sometimes."

Mom says awkwardly, "I told her she didn't have to come and work so hard. We'd manage on our own."

"She really shouldn't be on her own," says Jana. "Old people living alone—it's unsafe. The crime rate and all is terrible here in Chennai. Once she left the front door open all night. She could be murdered in her bed and we wouldn't even know." She collects herself and mumbles, "Your locker. I'll take care of it. Excuse me."

Mom and Lakshmi Auntie look at each other.

I whisper, "Mom, why won't Mami go stay with her son?"

Mom says, "I don't know."

Sumati says, "Mummy . . . ?"

Lakshmi Auntie says, quickly, "Shh, not now," because Mami's daughter-in-law returns with more papers. She is her composed business self again, and we have no time now to talk about an old woman with stories in her head who does as she pleases and won't listen to anyone.

Keeping an Eye on Things

❖ Picking up after Mami is starting to be a full-time job. She strings flowers into garlands for her pictures of gods, and forgets the thread and needle on the floor. She picks chaff from the rice and leaves both scattered on the dining-room floor.

I corner her in the garden one morning as she splashes the mopping water into the curry leaf plant. "Mami," I say, "can I ask you something?"

"Ask, ask," she urges.

"Are you all right? I mean, are you feeling all right?"

She swings the empty bucket in her hand. Drops of water fall from it, forming tiny instant craters of mud. She sets the bucket down and looks squarely at me. "Yes," she says, but her eyes are dark with secrets.

"Mami," I tell her. "You've been, you know, getting upset. Forgetting things."

For a moment her face looks as if it is about to crumple up. Then she recovers and whispers fiercely, "It's all right. I'm fine. Don't tell your mother."

I step back, startled. Again she says, "Don't tell your mother. I don't want to be any trouble to her."

"You're not—" I begin, but she interrupts me.

"Promise me. Promise me you won't tell her."

From habit, I mumble, "All right. I won't."

That afternoon, I find that the blue tote bag I have been using to haul my camera around is missing. I turn the bedroom upside down looking for it without success, then go down to ask my mother if she's seen it. She is in Thatha's office, shuffling papers and squinting at small print on faded forms. She runs her finger over the leather surface of the old desk, along the blurred gold vines trailing around the edge. But she is also somewhere else at the same time, checking details off on some list in her head.

"What's that?" She has flattened a piece of paper out on the desktop, and is looking at it so hard it seems she will burn it up.

She says in a whisper, "It's Thatha's death certificate. I had to make copies of it. What did you need, Maya?"

It strikes me suddenly. She misses her father. "Nothing," I say. "Nothing at all." I am embarrassed. I have intruded on a moment that was meant to be private.

Mami has washed the tote bag. It is a shriveled and shrunken thing now, flapping on the clothesline. I take it down and put it away in the closet with the rest of my stuff.

Unlike Dad, whose voice in my head is getting less and less reliable, and Mom, who doesn't have time to talk to me when I am right here, Kamala Mami has begun to talk loudly and at great length to people who aren't there at all. Actually, it's worse than that. She talks to people who are dead as if they were still alive.

I listen to her conversations. I flop onto my stomach on the broad wooden plank of the *oonjal*, and prop open a book. Sometimes I even read, and wait for the grumbling, rattling voice from the kitchen to blur its way into the stories I'm reading. From the *oonjal* I can peer into the kitchen when I want to. In this way, I watch Mami slipping into the world of her thoughts. It is like looking into one of those computer-screen savers where the desktop swirls away into a slow point of blackness, and then comes on in full color to start all over again. That's sort of how she is, making dark predictions one minute, and stirring up delicious treats the next. And every day I listen to her recite the names of the goddess, all 108, mine among them, slipping quickly away in the torrent of others. Her mind is on a peculiar journey of its own, and I get to run alongside.

It seems to me she lets it show more when I am around. To Mom, she is just Kamala Mami, eccentric and loud, and refusing to admit my mother is no longer a willful teenager. They bicker about everything, and especially about the house. Mom doesn't understand why Mami is working so hard at cleaning it when it's going to be sold. Mami says if she's going to see this house pass into the hands of strangers, she's going to give it to them clean if it takes her last breath. If Mom doesn't care what people think, she, Kamala, does, so will Prema let her go by, for the love of the gods, because the stairs need mopping again.

While she is arguing with Mom, Mami seems irritable but also normal. Or whatever is normal for her.

Every day I listen to her talking to Mom, and then, when Mom is out, when it is just the two of us in the house, she talks to herself. Sometimes from the way she looks at me, I think she knows I am listening.

Still, I watch her, learning to read the dips and dives of her behavior. One day she catches me off guard.

Mom has gone next door, to Mr. Rama Rao's house. Since we don't have a phone, she has to go next door every time she needs to call the bank or the realtor. Mr. Rama Rao often holds her up after she's done, bending her ear with weather predictions and complaints about the noise from the bus stop. The Rama Raos have fired their household help again, and Mrs. Rama Rao will need to vent about what she calls "the servant problem." So I know, because I too have been trapped in these conversations with them, that when my mother says, "I'm going to go make a phone call," it'll be forty-five minutes before we see her again.

I'm taking a bath when the doorbell rings. I hear the door open. Then I hear Mami saying something loudly, the same angry words over and over. I can't make out what they are. The door slams shut. The bell rings again, and then again.

But I am not really paying attention, for one small reason. It has four legs and a tail.

I haven't gotten used to sharing the bathroom with this gecko. I am afraid it will fall off the wall and drown in the bathwater or, worse, crawl across the ceiling, have a sudden heart attack, and fall on my head. So I make sure I keep an eye on it all through bath time. Sometimes it goes and hides behind the window curtains. That makes me really nervous because then I don't know where it is, and I become even more certain it will dart out from its hiding place to ambush me.

This bath does not involve a tub and suds. I take two buckets, one with cool water from the regular faucet, the one marked "cold," and one with boiling-hot water from a little heater thing that hangs on the wall and needs to be turned on half an hour before I begin the whole process. I mix the two buckets together, scooping with a big plastic container with a handle, until the water is a bearable temperature. I undress quickly, and pour scoopfuls of water over myself, stop and soap, then wash down again with more water. I do all this while trying to keep one eye on the gecko on the wall, which sometimes encourages me with startling and unexpected chirps. Its little translucent throat swells with the sound.

I brood about the gecko all through my bath, which is why I am not attending to Kamala Mami and the door. Even through the fog of steam from the bathwater, and the splash of it falling over me, though, it seems to me there's way too much shouting, and the doorbell rings a lot.

When the water in the bucket runs out, I turn it upside down and listen to the last gurgles draining away. I rub myself down with the big thin white towel, noticing I've grown taller. I glance in the mirror, all misted up from the steam, and someone strange stares back at me, her hair standing up in a cloud around her head, dark and smoky. Her eyes are big and shiny-brown, looking into mine so deeply she seems to be reading my jumbled thoughts. I stare, and as I stare my ordinary face swims back into focus.

I get dressed quickly and open the door, keeping careful watch to make sure the gecko stays out of my way. It chirps at me.

"What are you, trying to make friends?" I say. "Forget it."

Headlines and Stories

❖ "You did what?" my mother is saying when I get downstairs. "You sent Prasad away? Mami, he's the real estate agent. He's helping me sell the house."

Kamala Mami mutters and mumbles under her breath, then bursts out in explanation. Prasad isn't Prasad at all, she tells Mom, but a bandit called Malayappa who is wanted by the police.

"Police?" Mom shakes her head. "Mami, that's not so. You're getting him mixed up with someone else."

But Mami will have none of it.

"Oh, my lord," Mom mutters under her breath. "I go next door to make one lousy phone call, and she sends Prasad packing."

Mami brings an old yellowed newspaper from the

kitchen. She shows us the headline: SANDALWOOD SMUGGLER DIES IN EXCHANGE OF FIRE, and, in smaller letters below, FAMILY ACCUSES POLICE OF MISCONDUCT.

"There!" she declares, rustling the paper under our noses. "Look at him! He's a scoundrel. Look at his face!"

We look. The man in the picture has a mustache, and thick black hair, and a glint in his eye that shows up even in the blotchy newspaper photo.

"Prasad has a mustache," I tell Mom.

"Yes," she says. "But so do lots of men. And everyone here has thick black hair."

We are grasping for logic. There is none to be found.

Malayappa the sandalwood smuggler is dead. The article says so. He has been killed in a shootout with police. We point this out to Kamala Mami.

"Poor Prasad certainly doesn't look like a crook," says Mom. "He'd be really upset if he knew you thought he was a bandit."

Mami is unimpressed. "You can say what you like," she insists. "I know he is a scoundrel and a murderer. Don't let him try to tell you he will sell the house. He'll stick a knife in your back."

We stare at her.

"You don't know," Mami warns us. "These are terrible times." And she shows us other headlines to prove her point: BLAST SNUFFS OUT LIFE OF SCHOOLGIRL IN SRINAGAR; BOOTLEG LIQUOR SNUFFS OUT 13 LIVES IN CHENNAI; MISCREANTS FOUND HIDING IN TRAIN. It doesn't tell us if they got snuffed out too.

"See?" she says to us. "See?"

It doesn't seem to matter to her that Srinagar is three thousand miles north, or that some guys brewing toddy without a license couldn't possibly have anything to do with my mother's real estate agent. Mami is going to protect us from criminals and miscreants, and that is that.

In the afternoon she cooks up a perfectly wonderful meal while talking as fast as she can, and at the top of her voice. "They took you to jail!" she yells. "Because you wouldn't give your own gold wedding bangles for the white man's war. And you marched with the protesters, telling them to Quit India."

"Who?" I ask, in spite of Mom's warning frown.

"Oh, those people," says Mami, "those *vellaikkara*, they have a lot to answer for. You spent a day in jail for that protest, poor girl, and then you went again when they arrested people in 1945." And she belts out a few curses about the British. I listen with interest.

We get chapter two over the second course of rice and *rasam*. The *rasam* is delicious, sour and hot with tomatoes and black mustard seeds. "You both went to jail together to throw the white men out. You said, 'If Mahatma Gandhi can go to jail, we can go too. Nineteen years old and one of you unmarried even, the other a new bride! Such a terrible thing and yet so brave and wonderful. More *rasam*?"

I can't stand it. "Who?" I ask, even though Mom shakes her head, urging me not to get Mami any more worked up.

"Who? What do you mean, who?" Mami demands. "I ask you if you want some more *rasam* and you say, 'Who?' Your grandmother, that's who. And your grandfather's sister Lalli." And she dumps a ladle of *rasam* onto my rice, saying, "Eat, eat. You're too thin."

"Is that true?" I whisper to Mom when Mami goes to get more rice for us.

"Yes," she whispers back. "My mother and Thatha's sister used to go to freedom meetings. A lot of people did that. Civil disobedience."

I know about the freedom struggle that led to India's independence from British rule. I know that there were mass protests, burning British cloth, marching to the seaside to make salt in defiance of salt tax laws. But I had no idea my grandmother was involved in any of it. "She was arrested? Twice?"

Mom nods. "She got sick," she says. "I've always

heard it was something she picked up in jail. Typhoid, I think it was, but it left her quite weak and she never got her health back again. She died when I was very young, and no one ever talked much about it."

"I can hear you still," Kamala Mami continues, over the sweet *payasam*. "You tell me, 'Kamala, they let us out. They let us out because they are afraid. All together, we can topple an empire.' "

I say to Mom, "You never told me these stories about your family. I didn't know any of this."

Mami mutters and mumbles over the rest of our lunch. She has used up her story bag, it seems, and all she can give us now are incoherent snippets. She reels off the names of Indian leaders and British rulers of the freedom struggle days—"Gandhi–Patel–Nehru– Maulana Azad–Mountbatten–George the Fifth!" She murmurs snatches of freedom songs—

"Mere vatan ke logon
Zara aankh mein bhar lo pani."

Oh, people of my nation, fill your eyes with tears.

I know from the Culture Camp, where they'd taught us, yes, this very song, that Mami's Hindi is as heavy with her Tamil accent as my Tamil is weighed down by my American one. Language can make you a stranger in many places, but only if you let it. I find that com-forting, even while I feel Mami wandering beyond our reach.

After we've eaten lunch and put everything away, I notice Mami sits cross-legged by the screen door, click-ing and cracking her knuckles and staring out at the wash slab and the garden beyond. She's staring with a secret smile on her face, as if she can see something that the rest of us can't.

Mom sighs. "I'm worried about Mami. I think I'd better have a talk with Lakshmi about her. Maybe she needs to go see a doctor. Maybe there's something we can do to help her. Lakshmi might know."

I say, "Yes," and then I stop. I almost say, *Yes, yes. You're right. Something's the matter.* But then I remem-ber Mami imploring, "Don't tell your mother." So, I say nothing.

Mom gives me a curious look as she gathers up stray papers from the dining table and puts them in piles that line the walls of the drawing room. I get the sense that she is organizing her thoughts as she does this, making the house feel comfortable to her, like hanging friendship bracelets on the doorknob of my room does for me. The drawing room is starting to look like our house in New Jersey. I wonder if that is why Mami talks to the people in her life who are long dead—if it is her way of making a place comfortable, filling it with something of her own. But when you do that with paper and bracelets, people don't call you crazy.

"Maybe we need to call her family. Her son and his wife," says Mom.

It strikes me that Mami never talks about her family. Later, when I ask her about them, her face tightens. "They don't need me," she says. "They have their own lives." She grabs my hands and says, "Please. You must listen to me."

"What?"

"I have left my son's house. I will not go back. His wife hates me."

"What?" I am beginning to sound like a skipping CD.

Mami whispers urgently, "You mustn't tell anyone. She can't bear to have me live in their house. She reads my letters. She steals my money. I won't go back there. Please. Please don't make me." She is frantic, begging. "I would rather go to some temple and live on the charity of strangers," she says, "than go back to their house again."

"It's all right." I comfort her as best as I can. And I think, *All right? Maya, what are you going to do now?*

She says again, as she did before, "Please don't tell your mother or your Lakshmi Auntie. They'll make me go back there."

She droops in her old cotton sari, looking so distressed that I say quickly, "Mami! Look here. I need some help. Will you help me make some lime juice?" That distracts her and sets her mind on squeezing limes and stirring in sugar and water, and she says no more about her son. My mind is in a whirl. How can anyone treat Mami like that?

Auntie drops by the next day with Sumati and Ashwin, bringing us wheat *halwa* and crunchy *murukkus* from Grand Sweets Emporium. Mami leaves early, as she usually does on Friday, saying she has to go to the temple.

"You'll come back tomorrow, right?" I ask her. I worry that she might just decide to check in at the nearest temple. I think of the shaven-headed homeless old women who seem to live around large temples in the city. They eat at the temple kitchens and earn loose change from generous worshipers.

"Of course I'm coming back tomorrow," says Mami, suddenly herself again. "Why wouldn't I?"

I hang around, just in case Mom decides to talk to Lakshmi Auntie about Mami. Sumati tells me about a card-trick book her dad bought her. I can't listen. I need to buy time to think. I crunch my way through four rounds of crispy *murukku*. Lakshmi Auntie pointedly picks up the crumbs I scatter.

I eat so much wheat *halwa*, I begin to feel slightly bloated. I resist Sumati's efforts to get me to see her card tricks, and Ashwin's efforts to get both of us to listen to him recite funny poems. I want to know what's going to happen to Mami. I need to know. At the same time I don't want them to make any plans she wouldn't want to go along with. In addition, I've made my promise to her, and I must keep it. *Life's a mess, Maya-Preeta*, says the Dad voice in my head. I have to agree.

Mom tries to get rid of us. "Why don't you young people go up on the roof, or outside?" she says.

To which I cry, in desperation, "Oh, look at that man outside! He's peeing on the wall!" It's true. Some guy has decided he can't wait, and is using the outside of our garden wall for his bathroom.

Sumati smothers a laugh. Ashwin's eyes grow as big as lightbulbs. Lakshmi Auntie launches into a speech on the lack of discipline among India's masses and the growing number of unsanitary conditions in Chennai. She seems annoyed with me, as if I were personally responsible for these things. And Mom is so aggravated by my strange behavior that she gives me one of her "Maya-please-don't-interrupt-while-I'm-in-the-middle-of-a-conversation" talks. Pretty soon Lakshmi Auntie says they had better get going, and Mom ends up saying not one peep about Mami to her.

I have a frightful stomachache that night from all the wheat *halwa* I've eaten. It tempers my brief victory, and I begin to wonder if this is really a bigger problem than I can deal with.

Mami says she is all right. But she isn't. She won't go to her son's house, because her daughter-in-law hates her. Is Mami sick? Will medicine help her? I need to know. But I can't know, because I have promised Mami I won't tell.

Cyberconnexions

❖ The next day Mami keeps her promise, and returns. She has no stories to tell me. My mind is first restless, then undecided, then finally made up. True, I have promised Mami I won't tell Mom or Lakshmi Auntie a thing. I have not, however, promised her I won't tell Sumati. So I walk the two street lengths to Sumati's house, and share my dilemma.

She considers my story like a judge weighing the evidence. "All right," she says. "Let's think about this. The question is, is Mami okay, or should she go see a doctor? Right?"

"Right."

"And if she's sick, her son should take her to see one, right?"

"But she doesn't want us to tell him," I point out. "Because his wife hates her. And if my mom or yours found out, they would definitely call her son."

"Okay, fine. But a doctor would know if Mami's sick or not. Right?"

"Right." Can't argue with that logic, but how can we take Mami to a doctor? First of all, she won't go. Second, even with the money Sumati's aunt has sent her, we certainly don't have enough to pay for a doctor's visit.

We stare at each other. All at once, an idea strikes me. It is so perfect I feel faint from its brilliance. I say in triumph, "I know! Cyberconnexions!"

"The Internet place?" Sumati shakes her head in puzzlement.

"We can run a search," I tell her, "to look for information on what would make someone act like Mami."

We make our way to Cyberconnexions, with money we have scrounged up between us in hand. A few minutes later we stand in dismay, staring at the sign. It reads, SURF THE NET. RS. 35/- PER HOUR. We have only thirty rupees.

We are about to turn around and head back in defeat when the door opens and a friendly voice inquires, "May I help you, young ladies?" A white-shirted man with glasses waves us in. He is wearing a shiny brass name tag that says D. MOHANRAJ.

We explain our shortage of funds. "Will you need a whole hour, do you think?" he asks us. "Why not log on and I'll just charge you for the time you spend?" A coffeepot perks briskly on a small corner table. Cups, milk, and sugar are arranged invitingly for customers. A few people drift in and settle down at terminals. Some look like tourists, checking their e-mail, some like students. Modems hum, dialing up. Fingers click on keyboards. Screen-saver patterns zoom in steady rhythm on unused monitor screens. The place has its own heartbeat.

Within minutes, we are seated at one of the dozen computer terminals arranged against the wall. Mr. Mohanraj logs us in with flying fingers, and soon we have six possible search engines at our disposal. Eagerly, we get to work. We key in *memory* and *problems* and wait. In a matter of seconds, we are rewarded with three million plus hits, most of them having to do with memory problems on computers.

"Great! Now what do we do?" My terrific idea seems less brilliant now.

"How is it going? Everything all right with your connection?" Mr. Mohanraj hovers by.

We look at each other. Then in a rush the story of Mami pours out. I tell it, with Sumati adding details. To my ears my voice is high and nervous. I race to my conclusion. "And so we have to know, are we imagining things or is there something really wrong with her? Can you help us run a search that will tell us more?"

Mr. Mohanraj pulls up a chair. "How old is your Mami?" he asks. Sumati thinks eighty. I have no idea. He pulls up a Q-and-A site for us, hosted by a local hospital foundation, where people can find out about major illnesses. He types in a few words. *Memory loss, seniors, symptoms.* Soon we are reading about conditions that commonly afflict the elderly, illnesses with names like dementia and Alzheimer's disease.

After a while, the text begins to blur into a mass of meaningless words of many syllables. My head whirls with information overload.

Then, "Look!" says Sumati. " 'In Alzheimer's disease a pattern emerges over six months or more. The patient might routinely forget recent events, appointments, names, and faces.' Does that fit?"

"Some," I say.

She reads on. " 'He or she gets easily confused, suffers mood swings, bursts into tears for no apparent reason, or becomes convinced someone is trying to harm them or others.' Well, what do you think?"

"I don't know. It sounds really bad, and I don't think Mami's that bad, somehow."

"It says here," Sumati points out, "that 'there is no

single point in time when you can really tell it started. And after a while' . . ." She stops, and frowns.

"Yes?" I try to find where she's reading, and I stop too.

" 'After a while,' " she continues softly, " 'relatives of some patients say there are good days and bad days. On bad days they feel they are living with a stranger. The person they knew is simply not there any longer.' "

We sit there, stricken by the chilling thought, seeing together, because we have read together, the dreadful possibility that aging brings to some people. That Mami might be one of those people whose mind slowly decays. Then the phone rings on Mr. Mohanraj's desk, and we jump. It rings again and he answers it.

"Thirty-five rupees per hour." A pause. "We are open till nine-thirty." Another pause. Sumati and I say nothing to each other. "Yes, we have a superfast connection." Finally, he hangs up.

He walks over to us, leans on the desk. "If I might make a suggestion," he tells us, "I'd say you should take this lady to see a doctor. You can get some information here from Web sites, but you can't be certain." He points to a cautionary warning on the screen informing readers that the "information on this page is not intended to replace consultation with a licensed medical professional."

"Talk to your parents," he urges, "so you can take your Mami to see a doctor."

He charges us twenty rupees. I glance at the clock and realize we have been there for more than an hour. "But . . ." I begin. He waves us away. "It's all right," he says. "Never mind. Good luck."

Invisible Ribbon

❖ I fess up to Mom that evening. It takes her a while to unravel the threads of my account. "You what?" she says. "You and Sumati went and researched what? Where?"

"Dementia," I say, "except we think maybe it's Alzheimer's. Mom, it sounds really bad." I tell her about our trip to Cyberconnexions, feeling more and more foolish as the story unfolds.

She gets very quiet as I repeat the contents of the Web site as best as I can remember them. When I am done she says, "You're right. There is something wrong with her, isn't there? I've been wondering that myself for a while, wondering what we should do."

"We can take her to a doctor, right?"

"Well, we can. But first we have to get in touch with her son and Jana. I'll go talk to her at the bank tomorrow."

That is when we realize Mami is missing.

We look all over the house for her. She is not upstairs. She is not in the kitchen. She's not in the garden. She's vanished.

"Dear God," says my mother. "Now what do we do?"

I am struck by an inspiration. "Mom. Mrs. Rama Rao next door. Isn't she Mami's friend? Won't she know how to find her son? Maybe she'll have a phone number."

"You," says my mother, "are brilliant." She goes next door to talk to the Rama Raos. In a few minutes she comes back, all out of breath. "They don't have a phone, but Mrs. Rama Rao had a phone number of a neighbor of theirs. Her son's still not back from work. I talked to Jana. She's on her way. I think they live pretty close to here."

In twenty minutes, Jana arrives by auto rickshaw. She is understandably and loudly frantic. "*Ayyo*, what will I tell my husband?" she cries.

Mom tries to calm her down. "We'll go look for her. Don't worry. She can't have gone far."

We are spared the trouble. Mrs. Rama Rao scurries over, bursting with news. "You are looking for Kamala Mami? Lakshmi just phoned—she is in their house."

Pretty soon Lakshmi Auntie herself comes over. My head is starting to swim. The pace of this drama is electric. "You'll have to come and get her," she says. "She's refusing to leave until she talks to Maya. Should I take Maya back with me and you all wait here?"

Mom nods. "Come on, Maya," says Lakshmi Auntie, all businesslike. "Otherwise Mami's going to settle in for the night on Sumati's bed."

Jana wrings her hands. "This is terrible. What will four people think?" she says. The Tamil phrase is an odd one. I remember hearing it when I was younger. It was a favorite phrase of Ammamma's. It always puzzled me—what four people, and why should I care? Mami certainly wouldn't care what any four people might think.

When we get to Lakshmi Auntie's house, Mami is curled up on Sumati's bed, laughing to herself. Words tumble soft and fast and frenzied from her mouth. She pays us no mind, giggling in time to her own racing thoughts.

"See?" says Lakshmi Auntie helplessly. "I can't get her to listen to me. It's like talking to someone who isn't there."

Sumati's father, who is probably wishing he'd stayed

in Bangalore, tries to keep Ashwin occupied in his room. Sumati says, "Oh, thank goodness you're here. She's been shouting for you."

Mami cocks her head at me, the way some birds do when they're trying to judge if they should put up with humans nearby or fly someplace else.

"Okay," I say to Mami, "it's all right." I grab her hand. I sit on the bed next to her, and make her look at me. I hope I can get her attention. I hope she isn't too far off in her own thoughts to be able to listen to me. She mumbles to herself without stopping. I can't understand what she's saying.

"Shh," I say to her. "Shh."

She mimics me, finger to lips, smiling crookedly, playing along like a little kid.

"Mami, come," I tell her. "Come home with me."

But she is off on a journey of her own. "Home," she says. "Come home. Such a brave girl. Oh, look how thin you've become!" She looks at me, but she is seeing another face, another time.

Past and present have mingled in her mind. I decide that if I can't pull her from this world, maybe I can try to enter it. I say, "I know. It's terrible. But it's over now."

"Over?" She hesitates. "They let you go?"

"Mami." I'm talking slowly and carefully, knowing that the words I choose will either bring her into this moment of time or send her fleeing away. "It's over. It's all right now. Let's go."

She sighs as if there are dead-weight memory rocks in her heart, rocks made of unanswered questions, unresolved problems. The guilt of things said and done, of other words never spoken at all. She wavers between her worlds of inside and outside, then and now. At last she pulls her sari around her and gets up. "What are you people standing around for?" she says. "Go on! Nothing else to do?"

Relief floods the room in waves, washing over all of us. We go downstairs in single file.

We have one last hurdle to cross. Mami will not get in Lakshmi Auntie's car. She has decided Auntie is a spy. "German spy!" she says to her with a glare. "We'll shut down your bakery!"

"What?"

Sumati's dad explains this historical reference. "She's remembering the Second World War, when they closed down the German bakery in St. Thomas Mount because the British thought the owner was a spy. She's very confused."

"I am not confused," says Mami with dignity. "You are all traitors and spies!" She lunges at him.

I say, "Shh, Mami," and grab her hand in mine again. She quiets down, but refuses to ride in the car.

In the end, by flashlight and erratic streetlights, up

and down the uneven sidewalk, dodging homeless families settling in for the night here and there, I lead Mami home. Lakshmi Auntie drives on ahead of us, stopping from time to time to let us catch up with her, keeping an eye on us the whole way. Like burglars on the prowl, we walk in the darkness down St. Mary's Road to my grandfather's house. One old woman with crazy eyes, talking to herself, trotting along behind a girl who keeps a firm hold of her hand. If the late shoppers at the stores along the way think we look peculiar, they don't let on. They just make way for us. Like the people on the overcrowded buses here who make room for more passengers even when you can't imagine there is any more room to be made.

You'd think it was the most ordinary thing in the world, my leading an old lady down the road, my soul connected to hers with an invisible ribbon woven of stories and fragments of memory.

What Will Four People Think?

❖ Mami, despite having calmed down after our walk, refuses to go anywhere with her daughter-in-law. "I will take the number 45B to my room in Tambaram," she insists. It is so late, however, that the last bus to Tambaram has left.

"Maybe you should just stay here tonight," Mom suggests.

Jana pleads with Mami. "Why won't you come and stay with us? People will say we don't look after you, your own family, isn't it? That's what they'll say." From under the soft round mask of her face, Mami's daughter-in-law throws Mom a dagger of a look.

Lakshmi Auntie says, "Mami, they are your family. Why not go there, just for now?"

Even I, despite feeling like a traitor and a spy, add my voice. "We'll come and see you there, Mami."

Mami considers it all. Then she delivers her pronouncement. "When Sita sat imprisoned in the garden of the demon queen, she was still a princess."

"Why don't you come home with me?" Jana argues. "Don't you think we'll take care of you? Why are you working in other people's houses as if you had no family to support you?"

Mami doesn't miss a beat. "They tied a firebrand to Hanuman's tail," she snaps back, "and he ran through Lanka like a storm, burning the city up as he went." She pauses dramatically, eyeing her audience. "And Sita the goddess, Sita the gentle, Sita of the good heart, could see her rescue was at hand."

Not much we can say to that.

"All right," says Jana to Mom. "Let her stay here for the night. Tell us if anything goes . . . wrong. Tonight you can phone my neighbor if you have to. Tomorrow I'll be at the bank. My husband can come over in the evening. Yes?" Beneath the bluster there is a tremble in her voice.

"Yes, of course," says my mother.

Jana leaves, defeated.

Lakshmi Auntie offers to sleep over.

Mom agrees gratefully. Auntie pulls out her cell

phone to call her family and let them know they shouldn't expect her back. She says, "You should have a telephone handy anyway. Just in case." Just in case of what? None of us can imagine, since Mami in her right mind is unpredictable enough.

We camp out in the living room, where Mami has settled down for the night. She is curled up on a cotton rug spread out on the floor, in the enclosed porch between the kitchen and the garden. The cooling night air wafts in through the wrought-iron grille door. She is tired, and in a short time she is snoring like a freight train.

I go upstairs to get ready for bed. There is a small glow inside me. It comes from knowing that Mom and I have worked together to make things better for Mami today. It gives my steps a bounce. It makes me smile. As I turn the bathroom light on, the gecko scrambles up the wall. It gives me a warning chirrup. "Guess what?" I tell it. "You don't frighten me a bit."

When I go back down to the living room, I find that Mom and Lakshmi Auntie have made themselves comfortable. They've spread a few cotton rugs around, and created makeshift beds for the three of us. Lakshmi Auntie says, "Would you believe that Jana? So much more concerned with what four people will think than with what's going on with Mami?"

Mom says heavily, "We were all brought up with that, right? Always worrying about what others would say. Didn't you have to deal with that mentality, Lakshmi? With your in-laws?"

"Not as much as you," she says. "We've had our share of differences, who doesn't? But you, my dear. We should build a temple to you, what you've had to put up with."

I pretend to be occupied with fluffing up pillows.

"So many rules, so many restrictions," says my mother. "So many expectations. I didn't meet any of them. I was unprepared for it. It was never like that in our family."

She is digging into her past and unearthing episodes of which I am a part. The Dad voice in my head cautions me, *They're about to start on me. You know that, don't you?*

Mom has never talked about these things before, perhaps because there's never been anyone to talk to.

Sure enough, Lakshmi Auntie says, "Well, Ravi should have put his foot down, yes? He did marry you. So why didn't he tell his parents to leave you alone? I mean, interfering with everything! There's a limit. You couldn't name your own daughter, you couldn't make the life you wanted to."

Mom says, "Lakshmi, please."

I turn my face to the wall and try to get some sleep. But Lakshmi Auntie says, "Now, don't you 'Lakshmi, please' me. Does Maya even know what they'd planned for her?"

"Me?" I am instantly awake. Mom tries to evade the question, but I want to know. "Who? Planned what for me?"

Lakshmi Auntie shakes her head and says, "You never told her, right? I don't believe it."

For so long, we have allowed silence to grow and take over our family. Silence and secrets, promises from one to the other and back again, not to tell this or that to someone else. And I have been part of it too.

"When your father and I decided to separate," says Mom, finally, "his parents kept trying to tell him that it was all my fault, and that I was unfit to take care of you. They suggested that you go live with them."

"Me? Live with Ammamma and Rangan Thatha?"

"Yes. They had it all figured out. They would raise you because they thought you shouldn't be with me. They even sent a pair of plane tickets, one for you and one for your father."

"Dad said this was okay?" It hits me suddenly. "The letter . . ."

"What?"

That letter. That overnight letter that arrived the day

before we left. The one he made me promise not to tell Mom about. "The letter," I say. "It had tickets in it."

Now it is Mom's turn to look astonished. "You knew?"

I nod.

"He made you promise not to tell me?"

I nod again. My mother closes her eyes as if these memories are too hard to bear.

Lakshmi Auntie rolls her eyes. "You two," she says. "How long has it been since you've talked to each other?"

"They hardly even call anymore," I say.

"Too busy managing their bags of money," mutters Lakshmi Auntie. "It's all they cared about."

The ghost of my father, which has been getting blurry at the edges over the last few months, turns on its heel and walks out of my head.

All I can say is, "I wonder if that ticket was in my name or Preeta's?"

The Developers

❖ Mami is restless throughout the night, but we do manage to get some sleep. In the morning we find the city has wrapped itself in a haze that promises rain to come.

Lakshmi Auntie tells Mami she is going to arrange for her to see a doctor.

"What for?" Mami demands.

"Because at your age," says Auntie, "it's a good idea to go for a checkup. I'm going to phone your son, and he'll make an appointment for you, all right?"

Mami grumbles, but she agrees. It seems so simple.

Mom tells Mami to go ahead and take her bath in the upstairs bathroom. After she is done, I find she has splashed so much water about that the gecko has retreated to the farthest, highest corner of the room. Only its tail is visible from behind the hot-water heater.

We have visitors. Prasad brings along two suited men (from Tri-Star Development Private Limited) with briefcases and shiny gold watches.

They get down to small talk. They knew my grandfather, they say, and what a fine gentleman he was, and what a most excellent family we all are. They ask about me—"Your daughter, madam, she is how old now?" They swivel delicately around my father—"Madam, this property is in your name solely, as left to you by your late father, is it not?" "You and your daughter are living in the States? I see, I see." And on and on, circling, circling.

The talk moves to terms and agreements and something called a *patta*, which seems to be a sort of map the realtor says he has, and to advances and percentages and other technical points.

Mami offers coffee. To our embarrassment and the startlement of Prasad and the buyers, she has added salt to it instead of sugar. Mom apologizes, and says she'll brew a fresh pot. "No, no," they protest. "No need for coffee." She goes anyway.

Mami, irritated at her kitchen being invaded, accuses my mother at the top of her voice of being a Pakistani spy. Prasad tries to distract the developers, but they listen with interest. Mami is a solo theatrical performance. Mom calms her down with some difficulty, and manages to bring out fresh coffee, suitably sugared. Mami retreats to the garden with a large platter of lentils, and spends the next hour or so sifting through it for small stones and husks. Under her breath she curses spies, daughters-in-law, policemen, politicians, and several other groups of people.

After Prasad has left with his developers, we sit on the *oonjal*, exhausted. Mami has curled up on the floor and is snoring gently.

I ask Mom, "Are they going to buy the house?"

"They are," she says wonderingly. "It seems too good to be true. They're going to buy it and tear down the house and build a block of flats."

"Flats?"

"Apartments." There we go again, with the naming of things.

"Is that good?" I ask. "Tearing the house down?"

She shrugs. "It's okay. We can't live here. It's all right."

"You grew up here," I point out.

"Yes," she says. And then, "Well, you can't keep things like this forever. You can't live on memories."

Thinking about another house whose memories I have tried to live on, I say, "But houses aren't just houses."

She sighs. "True. They contain stories of people's lives, don't they? Like this house."

"Stories of Thatha's life? And yours?"

She nods. "But you have to move on."

"I don't see why you can't take the stories with you."

She gives me a surprised look. I continue, trying to keep my voice steady. "Just because we sold the house in New Jersey doesn't mean I have to forget all about the years we lived there, does it? All about Dad? Just like you don't have to forget this house, and Thatha."

A long pause stretches between us. Then she says softly, "No. Of course not."

I am beginning to see that the stories of people's lives are like the ocean waves Sumati and I watched at the beach, lapping endless shores, constantly moving, changing. This summer I feel filled to overflowing with Mami's stories, because of how alive they are, how deep and dark and scary-beautiful.

I say, "When you first went to America, was it hard to leave India behind?"

I know she is taken aback because she makes as if to brush the hair off her forehead when there isn't any out of place. She says, "I think it was, but not right then. It wasn't until years later I realized I missed it."

And then I have another question. "Mom, if you and Dad had stayed on in India do you think . . . you think you'd still be together?"

She says, "I don't know. I've often asked myself that. Maybe not, but it's hard to tell, and sometimes I think, what's the point of agonizing over such things? It doesn't undo them."

The *oonjal* creaks as we swing on it slowly. We sit together, missing our fathers.

Getting Help

❖ Mami's son comes that evening as promised. Except for his head of thick black hair, and the suspicion of a mustache on his upper lip, he looks just like Mami. He has her ready laugh. He has her gestures.

He tries to persuade her to go home with him.

"I can't," she says. "I have to stay here with Prema. When she came here to sell this house I promised her I would stay here and cook for her." She sets her chin, and will not budge.

He says, as if he's bargaining with a young child, "If we let you stay here tonight, will you come with me to see a doctor tomorrow?"

Mami waves him away with a little laugh. "We'll see. Tomorrow. All right, all right. Go home. It's getting late."

"Poyittu varain," he says, the Tamil goodbye that really means "I'll be back." But before he can keep his word the next day, Kamala Mami falls apart like a stack of papers in a good stiff wind. And she is not laughing.

The day is hot and still. On her way out to check the mailbox, Mom has no doubt been trapped by Mr. Rama Rao, and is deep in a meteorological discussion with him. I go to the dining room to get myself a glass of water from the refrigerator that stands against the far wall. That's when I see her.

The moment I set eyes on Mami I know this is beyond anything I've ever seen before. She sits in a corner, bunched up close to the ground. And she weeps as if her heart is breaking. She makes no effort to cover her face or turn away. She just sits there and cries in long soft sobs.

"Mami," I say.

"I couldn't keep my word," she says. Over and over. "I told you I would take care of your daughter. How did I know she would go so far away? How could I know?" She can't hear me, see me.

Think, Maya. No time to dawdle. I stand there, watching her the way I watch a horror movie—can't look, but can't bear not to look.

"What a life she's had," she cries. "What a terrible, terrible life."

It's impossible to keep a single thought in my head long enough to become a decision.

Mami cries louder, in long jagged breaths, as if her lungs can barely fuel the sadness bursting out from inside her. I can practically see them, the ghosts in her brain that are making this happen. I see that I was right to be afraid for her, back when I first suspected something was wrong.

No time to dawdle. I run down the hallway, fling the front door open, and race outside barefoot, not caring that the gravel hurts my feet.

Mom is nowhere to be seen. She must be inside the Rama Raos' house. I hesitate a moment. Should I go in there and get her? Then I remember the words of Mami's daughter-in-law: "Tell me if anything goes wrong." I know what I need to do.

I head for the corner of C. P. Ramaswamy Road and the cross street with the police station and the tree with the trunk as big as a house. I take this road in the longest strides and biggest gulps of breath I can manage. The next cross street houses the bank.

Inside the Union Bank I search the faces. From behind the counter where she's handing papers to a teller, Mami's daughter-in-law meets my eyes in startlement. She whispers something to the woman she's working with and ducks out to talk to me.

I say, all breathless, "It's Mami. You need to come. Now."

She says, "Wait here." She returns in a moment, purse in hand. "It's all right," she says. "Let's go."

Only when I get back to the house with Jana do I realize I'm still barefoot. My feet are filthy. Perhaps Ganesha kept an eye out for me, the way I've tried to keep watch over Mami. I could have stepped on nails or broken glass and not even known it.

I leave Jana alone with Mami, and go upstairs. I quickly pour water over my poor feet, and rub them against each other. The water is dark brown as it washes the dust of the street away. The gecko's nowhere in sight.

We get ready to take Mami to the hospital. Mom, surprised out of her conversation with Mr. Rama Rao, goes to wave down a taxi for us. I stay with Mami while she sits and gazes into the distance, recognizing no one. Her daughter-in-law stares as if she is seeing her for the first time. Mami's tears have stopped flowing now, but every once in a while a tatter of a sob still breaks free from her. Sometimes her hands clasp and unclasp, fluttering like monstrous moths, and then are still again.

I am grateful when Mom returns, telling us she has

a taxi waiting outside. It takes all our combined strength, Mom and me and Jana, to get Mami into the cab. For once, Mr. Rama Rao is at a loss for words. He sits on his porch and watches us openmouthed.

At the hospital, the three of us and a doorman have to get her out and into the building. She fights like a cat.

The hospital is crowded. Once we have her inside, Mami becomes still. She will not look at us. A nurse shuffles patients in and out of examining rooms behind green curtains. When it's Mami's turn, she goes without a fight.

A resident tells us they will probably transfer Mami to an observation ward. Mami's daughter-in-law is in a daze. "We'll have to run a series of diagnostic tests," says the resident, with the air of one who has explained everything perfectly. "Are you relatives?"

"I am," says Jana, and so of course he turns to her and ignores us completely.

"Will she be all right?" Jana asks.

"Don't worry." The resident adjusts the stethoscope hanging around his neck. "Come tomorrow. By tomorrow we might be able to tell you more."

In the evening, Jana and her husband both show up at Thatha's.

"I'm so sorry," Mami's son says. "So much inconvenience you've had to put up with."

"It's all right," replies my mother. "What will you do now?"

He shrugs and smiles. "I will take her home with us when they discharge her from the hospital. She has always insisted she can manage on her own . . . " He trails off, and then says, "Thank you. Thank you for taking care of her." He aims the words at Mom but he looks right at me.

I think of Mami cooking for us, telling stories I can hear from my place on the *oonjal*, singing for herself and no one else. Mami in a rage when she was sure Prasad the real estate man was a murderer wanted by the police, an ax-wielding maniac out to get us. Mami reciting the names of the goddess, all rattly like pebbles rolling down a mountain.

And I feel sad. Oh, not for Kamala Mami. She carries worlds around in her imagination, and why would I need to be sorry for someone who has that? I feel sorry for myself because I won't have her around anymore, and I am fiercely jealous of the people who belong to her, as I do not.

The Book

✧ The smell of disinfectant in Mahila Hospital is unimaginable. It hits us as we walk in the following morning. It is so thick it goes up my nose and lodges in my sinuses. I have the feeling I'll be able to smell it years from now, when I am far away from this place where silk cotton trees make umbrellas over the courtyard outside, and where, inside, the walls are busy with white and green tiles.

We check in at a counter, where a man in a blue uniform writes our names down twice, once on a form and once in a ledger. I wonder what they'll do with the names of all the visitors who come to see the patients in this rambling red brick building. Will anyone ever read them again? Jana arrives and I snap out of my daydream.

A nurse's aide in a green sari, almost matching the tiles but not quite, leads us to the observation ward. She turns us over to a nurse at the desk. "Is she expecting you?" The nurse bites her words out.

Mom dithers. Jana says, "I am her relative."

"And you?" Nurse Barracuda glares at us.

"They're friends of the family," says Jana.

The nurse points us to a waiting room and says, "Wait there. I'll bring her to you."

Pretty soon she reappears with Kamala Mami. Jana talks to her in the loud voice people reserve for those who are deaf, foreign, or a little slow. She pronounces each word clearly and carefully. "How. Are. You?"

Mami digs in the folds of her sari and extracts something. "What. Is. That?" enunciates her daughter-in-law, tugging her sari around herself, *whoosh-whoosh*.

Mami jerks her head at me, away from everyone else. I sit down next to her. "What?" I ask. "What is it?"

It's a little accordion-folded book with parchment-like pages bent from age and use, Tamil letters rolling across the front.

"I want you to have this," she whispers to me. "Lakshmi Sahasranaman. Your name comes from there, Maya. Mahamaya. Remember that." She opens it, and shows me, ம - ா - ய - ா, m-a-y-a. She presses the book into my hands and leans back, exhausted.

Kamala Mami and I sit and stare companionably at

the little book. My name in there! I speak, finally, and to my surprise the silence doesn't shatter the way silence is supposed to. It just parts and makes way for what I have to say. "Are you sure you want to give me your book? Won't you need it?"

She smiles, and says, "I have another one, don't you worry." With a shock of pleasure I realize it's a Two-Gift!

She nods encouragingly at me and waves the little book away. I slip it into my tote bag, tucking it between my camera and my wallet.

I take her rough hand and hold it, wanting to smell familiar smells of flowers and hair oil and diesel fumes from the bus, but I smell only hospital disinfectant.

"You should go home," I say.

"Home," agrees the nurse from the doorway. "She'll go home soon. She's so much better." She beams at us, barracuda transformed into angelfish. *"Illai, ma,* Kamala? Isn't that so, dear?"

But Kamala Mami doesn't answer. Instead she pats my hand with her dry-as-dust ones. Then she leans over and says to me, "What a terrible thing, to take a young girl like you to jail," and I realize that her mind has gone off on its journey to the past again.

I take a picture of her, although my hands shake so I can barely hold the camera straight. She gives a crooked grin, then asks Mom to take one of her and me together. I sit next to her, and try to smile, wondering who she thinks I am. Mom aims and clicks. The flash goes off in a little explosion of brightness, leaving small bursts of color whizzing about in my eyes.

"The house?" she asks Mom, and I see she is back in our reality.

"Prasad's still talking to buyers," Mom tells her. They look at each other a long time.

Finally Mami waves her hand like an empress dismissing her subjects. "Sell it," she commands. "It's only a house. The real remembering—it's inside." She thumps what Sumati would call her boozum.

I open my mouth to say something to Mami. Goodbye, maybe? Good luck? What can I possibly say?

She spares me the trouble of figuring it out. She leans over and whispers so close in my ear her warm breath tickles, "Sometimes people leave our lives. It isn't a thing to cry about."

I shush, humbled. What do I know? She is an ocean of story, filled with answers to questions I have barely begun to ask.

The Woman on
the Escalator

❖ A week goes by so slowly it gives me the prickles, like when you sit on a folded leg too long. Mom waits to hear from Prasad, who is waiting to hear from the Tri-Star Development people about when they need to go to the registrar's office for one last meeting about the house. The Tri-Star people take their time because they are waiting to get a good date for the meeting— from their astrologer.

"Astrologer?" I ask. "Really? Why?"

She nods. "Just a custom, that's all. They'll call Prasad when they have a date."

"Perfectly normal," Sumati reassures me. "You never begin a thing without consulting an astrologer." Lakshmi Auntie mutters something about that being the whole problem with India because how can you make any progress when you can't even hiccup without having to get the astrologers to pick a good day for it.

At last the meeting happens. Finally—yes!—the house is sold. Prasad shows up with sweets to celebrate. Mr. Rama Rao leaves his post on the porch to come and talk to him. "Prasad, my good friend," he cries, and hurries over to shake his hand so hard the change in the real estate agent's pockets rattles. "And how is the market treating you these days?" I wait for him to move into a discussion about the weather, but instead they talk about the old days when Mr. Rama Rao was the person to go to in the High Court for the special "stamp paper" you needed for legal documents.

"That's what you used to do?" I say. "I wondered why you'd work at the High Court selling stamps." It's a mistake. I get a half-hour lecture on the fine points of stamp paper and the importance of getting the right value of it for various things, wills and bonds and sale deeds. Mr. Rama Rao imparts this knowledge as if he is sharing valued truths with me. Prasad says a hasty goodbye and goes into the house to talk to Mom.

Mr. Rama Rao's wife comes out and gives me some more sweets because their grandson has just turned six, "and you will not get these real Indian sweets in

America, no?" She regales me with the latest on the domestic-help front. "All is well. Radha is back working for us. She has two little kids. When you go back to America, you must send them some nice pens and pencils they can use in their school, all right? We must do what we can to help uplift these poor people." I promise to do my bit, and eat sweets until the charge of sugar makes my head spin. I am rescued by a blood-curdling scream that comes from inside the Rama Raos' house.

"No worry," says Mrs. Rama Rao, seeing my startled look. "Tea kettle. Raoji says world coffee-bean prices are going sky-high, so we are switching to tea." She hurries off to take care of the shrieking kettle, and I make my escape.

The talk of stamps reminds me that I owe Joanie her postcard to go with the Two-Gift. I pick one from the lot we bought at the bookstore. I write a few lines on it, address it, and tell Mom I'm going to go mail it.

"Now?" she asks. "You'll probably get home before it does."

I didn't want to come in the first place. I should be pleased to be going back. But I'm not. I'm as mixed up as Mami's memories. "I guess," I mumble, and slip out the door to go mail the postcard, never mind if I get there before it does.

I pass the tea stall, the bus stop, and another row of shops. At the barbershop (HAIR CUTTING RS. 20/-, CHILD CUTTING ONLY RS. 10/-) I cross the street to get to the mailbox. It's bright red and looks more like a giant fire hydrant than a mailbox. I slip my letter in. I drag my feet back to the house, thinking of Kamala Mami. She's with her family, probably giving her daughter-in-law a hard time. I am smiling, thinking of her, when a woman hurries past me on the sidewalk.

It is one of those times you're so close to someone your eyes connect without your meaning them to. To my astonishment, I recognize the woman whose sari the escalator ate up outside the bookstore. There is no question, it is the same woman. I stared at her quite a bit when she was getting mauled by the escalator. What I don't expect is that she'll recognize me. She doesn't say anything. But her eyes meet mine for a long moment, then tear away with such a look of embarrassment and dislike that it hits me like a slap in the face.

Why? What did I do? I want to say, *What was so terrible anyway? It wasn't your fault. And it wasn't my fault, was it, that the stupid machine decided to strip off your clothes?* Of course, you can't stop perfect strangers in the street and tell them things like that, so once we break eye contact, she brushes past me.

The street kicks into fast-forward. The mango seller swears at someone who has jiggled her cart and loosened the brick placed under a wheel to hold it steady. The tea-stall owner shoos away the yellow dog that hangs around waiting for scraps. A bus stops suddenly and sets clouds of dust swirling. A pair of kids on bicycles race each other up the road, ringing bike bells as hard as they can, *trrring-trrring-trrring!* In an instant, the woman is gone. The crowds have closed right around her, as if I've imagined it all. But I haven't.

I remember Mami looking at me like that, not wanting to be spoken to, not wanting me to stop the voices in her head. And faintly, very faintly, there is a picture of someone else shooting a look like that at me.

"I want to stay here with you!" I'd cried in desperation. "I don't want to leave this house. Why do I have to?" But my father had become a very different father from the one I'd loved, the one who'd read to me and helped me with nosebleeds and made me laugh. He had pushed me aside, saying only, "You will have to talk to your mother about that." Then he'd gone down to his office and slammed the door. Soon afterward Mom and I moved out.

Crossing the road, while skirting the place where laborers are digging a big hole in the ground for water pipes, I begin to see these things again. And they are not what I have thought them to be. The look in the woman's eyes was her own embarrassment. It was never about me.

And the look in Mami's eyes? Well, that had nothing to do with me. I just happened to be there to see it.

My parents? There are things about them that I am only beginning to understand.

I lean on the gate in front of Thatha's house, push it open, and marvel at how treacherous memories can be. Mami no longer controls hers. I wish I could erase a few of mine.

Mr. Rama Rao calls out to me, " 'If water is rationed, city will make it through summer.' Right here in *The New Indian Express*."

I smile at him, wondering at how just being here, in this maddening, dazzling place, makes so many bits of my life fall together like a giant puzzle.

My Fault

❖ The next day the entire tribe of my mother's family descends on us with one long shriek. At least it seems that way. The cars begin to arrive at six o'clock in the evening, and swiftly fill the gravel driveway. "Are we having a party?" I ask Mom.

She says a little breathlessly, "It's all my cousins."

Within fifteen minutes, I am surrounded by relatives. I am drowning in conversations that compete for my attention. Two startlingly identical little boys (known together as "Rajeev-Sanjeev," or sometimes "the twinlets") play happily among my river of rocks in the garden. They hijack the shoes and slippers everyone's taken off at the door, and arrange them carefully on the rocks like a strange flotilla of ships.

I ask Sumati, "What's the occasion? How come everyone's here all at once?"

Sumati shakes her head, and I can't tell if she's giggling because the noise level has been ratcheted up several notches. She says, "No, no special occasion. Just a family get-together."

"Do you have them often?"

"Actually, no," she says. "But they all know you're leaving. Some of them have been to see you already, right?"

"Right." I nod and smile at those I can recognize. And I find that I too want to meet all these people, so many of them just names tossed about by Mom and Lakshmi Auntie. An elderly woman in a sapphire-blue silk sari exclaims, "Prema, we're so lucky you came to town! This family never gets together! Takes someone visiting from America to pull us all into the same room." To me she says, "Oh, little Maya! You don't know me but you can call me Ra Auntie. Everyone does."

The air is filled with simultaneous exclamations from people delighted to see one another. "Ajit! A married man! So where's the generous girl who gave up her life to take you on?" "Prema, you should have been at Ajit's wedding! His wife's a Star TV commentator, you know. Couldn't take a step at that wedding without tripping over one media celebrity or another."

Weddings, births, birthdays, college entrance exams—they fly by fast and furious in this cross fire of talk. Sumati whispers to me, "Watch, they're going to start on you in a minute."

Sure enough, in a little while there is a lull in the conversation. They pause, only until someone's eye alights on me. As one, they all cry out, "Maya! You've grown so big. Remember when you cried at seeing Lakshmi's husband, Kullan, for the first time?"

"Actually," I say, "I don't remember that. But I'm sure it's true because everyone says so."

"Maya, darling," says Priya, the mother of the twins, doing her best to restrain her energetic offspring. "You'll soon find out if you don't know already, if this bunch agrees on anything they tell you, it's probably totally untrue." She's drowned out by a chorus of protests, agreement, laughter, and questions. "Oh, well said!" "What? What nonsense!" "Now, now, Priya, you always had a sharp tongue in your head." "Where's Kullan, anyway? Traveling again, huh?"

To watch my mother in the middle of this is like viewing an elaborate show in which dancers come together in constantly shifting groups.

And oh, the food they have all brought. There is *aviyal*, with tender vegetables swimming in a light and delicate coconut and green chili gravy. Tamarind rice, sour and hot at the same time, with fried nuts hiding flavor surprises in random bites. Yogurt with grated cucumber, garnished with popped mustard seeds, to counter the heat.

"This food reminds me of something," I say.

The famous Raji, who defied her mother to go to architecture school, has the answer. "It's all Mami's influence," she says, with the air of one who means, *Can't you tell?* "Who do you think has left traces of her cooking magic in every single kitchen in this family?"

Ra Auntie (I find out her younger sister, in green, is called Ro Auntie) explains, "When Mami used to work in your grandfather's house, all of us old ladies were young like you, and we knew where the best food was to be had."

"But she didn't teach all of you to cook, did she?" asks Sumati the practical.

Ro Auntie chimes in, "Great cooking, my dear, can't be taught. But great taste can be cultivated, and you know, Mami's the best! None of us can help it—we keep trying to reach for that special touch! Come on, come on, everyone eat!"

It's true. This food has come from a dozen different homes. It's been cooked by a dozen different hands. Yet Mami's signature lingers in every bite.

So I miss her. But is that why I fall apart?

157

The twins are the immediate cause. Ashwin's playing big brother and making paper chains for them. They laugh and lug a long, growing-longer chain around the room. In the process of playing, it gets wound around the dining table. One end of it gets trapped by the leg of a chair. One of the twinlets, Rajeev, or maybe it's Sanjeev, gets all droopy around the mouth.

With the best intentions, I offer to help. "I'll get it for you." I make a dash for the table, at the exact moment that Lakshmi Auntie emerges from the kitchen, carrying an enormous bowl of *payasam*. In a superb display of klutziness, I run right into her.

In dreadful slow motion the bowl capsizes. A wide white river of *payasam* spills out onto the floor.

"Oh, Maya!" cries my mother.

My hands are sticky from my unsuccessful effort to recover some of the spilled dessert. "I'm sorry! It was an accident." My voice sounds shrill, on the brink of losing control.

Mom murmurs, "It's all right." She smiles, that bright, bright smile that is meant to keep peace at any cost. But it won't this time. It can't, because words are pouring out of me so fast I don't even know where they're coming from.

"No. You always do this. Make like everything's all right when it isn't. Smile and carry on. You've done it for years, Mom. You did it when Dad went away and you can't, I mean, I can't!" I am shouting and I can't stop myself. This is about as public a place as I can pick for this, and I know she hates it and I hate it and I don't care. Don't. Care. All I know is that this is it. We have to stop pretending everything's all right, but we also have to pick up our lives, and stop wishing for magic to happen. Here and now is what counts. It's the only thing. I am a wave of words, crashing, pounding, on a wide flat beach.

The wave has dashed over my mother, knocking her breath away. We both know this isn't about spilled *payasam*. My face grows hot and tears come streaming down my cheeks.

The hubbub of family conversation, the clamor of plates, the chinking of cups, all seem to stop, and there is only us, pooling our old unspoken anger under the rhythmic swishing of the ceiling fan.

"Oh, my God," says Lakshmi Auntie.

"I tried and tried to make it all right," I said. "I tried so hard. You weren't even there half the time. You're still not there for me. You're so busy planning for tomorrow, you don't know when today's just about gone." I can hear my voice. It sounds like somebody else's. "All I am for you is trouble. Ever since I was born, I've been nothing but trouble."

The silence is thunderous. It is like that moment you get when the power goes out, a tiny sigh of time before all the electric appliances in the house click quietly and shut themselves off. Then, as if on cue, the twinlets burst into synchronized tears.

Like an army galvanized into action, the family moves in on the trouble spot. They pick up and comfort the little guys. They roll up their sleeves and get to work. They mop. They soothe. They sweep. They scrub. They clean up. They rid us of that offending spill in a matter of minutes, and they do it all under cover of a barrage of banter and advice, offered up at top volume.

And then, quite suddenly, it's done. They leave as swiftly as they arrived, in a flurry of jasmine-scented goodbyes. Lakshmi Auntie, Sumati, and Ashwin are left with us.

Sumati says, "You're going to be gone so soon. Then we'll be back to me and the Pest."

Ashwin's so tired from chasing the twinlets, he can't do more than grin.

She says, "Send me an e-mail when you get back, okay?" She scribbles her e-mail address on a scrap of paper, folds it into an impossibly tiny square, and thrusts it in my hand.

I nod. We go out to see them off.

"Lakshmi," says my mother sometime during the last round of hugs. "Did you call everyone? Did you engineer this gathering?"

"I'm not admitting to anything," says Lakshmi Auntie.

Naming Maya

❖ We fall into bed exhausted that night. Another hot day goes by, and people arrive to buy the furniture, leaving only two beds for us to sleep in. They'll come back for those after we've left. A music collector scoops up a stack of old 78-rpm records. He is a friend of Mr. Rama Rao's. "Oh, thank you," he says over and over. "This collection will have a good home, I assure you." Even piles of old magazines and newspapers are weighed and sold. A van with "Seva Ashram" on it in red letters hauls off boxes of old clothes for the homeless. In all the flurry Mom and I have no time to say two words to each other.

The day after the house has emptied, the rains arrive in the city. The clouds burst suddenly. The hot earth gives up the smells it has hoarded all summer, and in minutes the gutters rush in torrents, and the gaping construction holes fill with swirls of red mud. The *kuyils* in the mango tree grow frantic with delight. So does Mr. Rama Rao. He runs outside into the storm, wearing a woolen scarf wrapped around his head. He waves his newspaper, proclaiming to anyone willing to listen, "Oh, I say, very good, southwest monsoon is here! I was telling you all, we will get rain in Chennai this summer!"

The house feels abandoned without the furniture, without the commotion of relatives gossiping and joking and taking verbal potshots at one another. Without Mami singing in the kitchen, clanging pots and pans to drive away the crows. There aren't even any crows—they are probably hiding somewhere, trying to stay dry. I miss the smell of incense in the house. I go to the dining room where Mami's little shrine still sits in its niche in the wall. I pick up the packet of incense sticks, "Jyothy Agarbathi Sticks" in bright red lettering on the barrel box, and light one. The match scratches and flares and soon the sandalwood scent is thick.

I trudge upstairs, thinking I should begin packing my stuff for the next day's flight. I gather up all my rolls of film and put them away in my suitcase. I turn around and see Mom standing in the doorway, watching me.

"Put as much as you can into the suitcase," she says. "That way you'll have less to carry on board."

"Okay." But she doesn't check me off and go on with the next thing on her list. She keeps looking at me.

"What?" I say, getting squirmy.

She says, "A cat may look at a king, right?"

The phrase is an old joke. Thatha used to say that. I'd catch him smiling to himself and looking at me, and I'd say, just like now, "What?" He'd make me laugh with that cat-king line. I'd ask, "Who's the cat? Who's the king?" And he'd say, "Now, that, your majesty, you have to decide."

We laugh now, and then I say, "I'm no king. Look how I ruined your party. Some royal behavior that was."

"It's all right," she says, coming into the room. "I don't think anyone really minded." She sits down on the bed and straightens out a suitcase strap that has twisted around itself. "You were dramatic," she says, "but you got my attention. And that's a good thing, because maybe I just haven't given you enough of it lately."

It's my turn to stare at her, then slowly I continue to put things into my suitcase.

A hundred thoughts from this strange, sad summer hammer in my head like the rain on the pavement. I pick up Mami's Two-Gift book from the floor where I have put it, thinking I will pack it away as well. As I do so the yellow silk cord that holds it together comes undone. The accordion-folded pages flip open. Papers flop out of the book and spill all over the floor.

I pick one up. Mami has hoarded photographs in the book, tucked them into a little pocket on the back page. "Oh, my," says Mom.

My mother's younger self, six or seven years old, with a round face and a set chin, looks curiously out of a yellowing picture at us, as if she too wants to know about this business of family secrets and what to do with them, when to keep them and when to give them away. She clutches a doll in one hand. The doll stares into the camera, a smile painted on its face.

"It's very unfair," I say.

"What is?"

"The way things change." I know Mom has questions, but she does not ask them. She just waits. She offers me a silence that is really an invitation.

"Mami," I say. "We needed to take care of her, and yet there was a time when she took care of you."

She nods. "Things changed with us too, didn't they? You, me, your father." There. It is simple and true.

Things change. She says, "I married someone who was funny and smart and charming. I don't know what happened. Maybe he changed, or maybe it was me. But there you were, caught between us. You were such a tough little kid. Such a will you had, trying so hard to hold us together. I couldn't stand to see you torn in two because we were unable to carry on. At some point I began to realize the marriage was a promise I had to break."

She knew, then. She knew about me in the middle. Me between parents, between grandparents, between names. Between promises made and kept like Two-Gifts. But in the end, you can't live your life by them, because people come and go. *Payasam* spills, and you can't keep trying to cover it all up. Sumati would say, "It's how it is." Joanie would say, "Just do what's right and it'll be okay."

When my parents split up, it never occurred to me that Mom needed caring for too. She planted a perpetual smile on her face and kept on going. She went to graduate school. She got a degree. She got a job. I lost her to all those things. She did what she could for me, dropped me off and picked me up from piano lessons and soccer, came to parent-teacher conferences. She did all the things she had to do, so I never knew how she felt about it all inside.

We share this thing that has happened in our family, Mom and me. It is not good or bad that we share it. It just is. The only bad thing is we never talked about it.

Mom says, "You'll still have the last couple of weeks of your summer vacation, before school starts."

I say, "Yes." Hanging out with Joanie, going to the pool. It's all only days away, but it's also a whole world away. A shrinking world, however. "Sumati gave me her e-mail address," I say. "I promised I'd send her a message when we get back."

"What a good idea," she says. "It's wonderful you get along so well."

"Maybe we can come back and visit them again some other time."

"Maybe," she says, "or they might come visit us." Maybe. No guarantees, but there's that world, growing smaller again. I could spin it on the tip of my finger. Just sitting here, talking about possibilities, is an amazing thing. She says, "So this hasn't been such a dreadful trip for you after all, has it?"

I think of Mami, and Sumati, and Ashwin with his little-kid jumpiness, and Lakshmi Auntie with an opinion about everything. And Mr. Rama Rao going on about the weather, and his wife with her endless stories about servants. I listen to the rain thundering down outside, and it feels as if the land is getting the good scrubbing wash it's needed for so long. I say, "No, it hasn't been dreadful. Not at all."

"You've been a great help to me," she says, "and to Mami. You made it possible for us all to help her."

"Is she going to be all right?"

"Some days yes, and other days maybe no. Her memory might go on getting mixed up."

It seems so unfair that such a thing should happen to someone with so many stories to tell.

But then Mom smiles. "I think she's going to keep her son and daughter-in-law on their toes," she says.

"She'll keep them hopping," I agree. We laugh, and it's as if some of Mami's laughter has touched us.

I think of something else. "Mom, do you suppose I should send Dad some pictures from this trip? Think he'd want to see them?"

I watch for a shadow to cross her face. I add quickly, "You know—I thought he'd like to see some of the better ones."

"Sure," she says. "I don't see why not." We are silent for a moment. The only sound is rainwater pouring off the roof gutters. Then she goes off to pack, and I turn back to my suitcase. Pretty soon, it fills up with clothes, and toiletries, and a few books I have salvaged from Thatha's old shelves. Finally, I pack two wads of tissue paper. Each contains a small baby elephant carved in wood, with a curving trunk and large, friendly ears.

It's a Two-Gift, trust. You keep some, you give some away.

Author's Note

The city of Chennai is in the state of Tamil Nadu, in southern India. The language the people speak there is Tamil. Many of the Tamil words in this book are included in the glossary, even though most of them are understandable from the context of the story. Maya is raised in the United States and she knows some Tamil, but when people talk fast she's sometimes a bit lost, so she figures out some words by asking questions, and others by doing some quick guessing. That's not a bad way to learn a language! After all, when you listen to a piece of music, it's possible to hum along even when you don't grasp all the words.

A few of the words Maya and her family use are not Tamil but Hindi, a language of northern India whose words have crept into use all over the country. Others are English words commonly used in India, but without the same meaning that they have in the United States. That is because British English was used in India during two centuries of colonial rule. Since independence, people in different parts of the country, including Chennai, continue to put their own stamp on the English language.

Tamil Glossary

(Pronunciation guide: "th" indicates the sound as in the word "thick"; "<u>th</u>" underlined is pronounced as in the word "they." All syllables in Tamil are equally stressed.)

akka (uhk-kah): big sister.

appalaam (uhp-puh-lahm): fried or roasted lentil crisp-bread.

aviyal (uh-vee-yuhl): stew made with vegetables in a coconut-and-yogurt sauce.

ayyo (ay-yoh): exclamation, similar to "Oh, dear."

bajji (buhj-jee): vegetables dipped in gram-flour batter and fried; a snack food.

chappals (chuhp-puhls): flip-flops.

Devi (<u>th</u>ey-vee): the goddess in any of her various forms.

Durga (<u>th</u>oor-gah): a fierce goddess created from the combined energies of the gods.

Ganesha (guh-nay-shuh): the elephant-headed god of Hindu tradition.

ghee (ghee): clarified butter.

halwa (huhl-vah): sweet dish made with wheat, Cream of Wheat, or other ingredients, often spiced with cardamom and saffron.

Hanuman (huh-noo-mahn): monkey god in the Hindu tradition.

illai (ill-lie): no.

Kali-yugam (kuh-lee-yoo-guhm): the age of sinners, the last age before the final destruction of the universe, after which the cycle begins all over again.

kameez (kuh-meez): loose tunic worn over *salwar*. A northern Indian dress now common everywhere in India.

kanna (kuhn-nah): affectionate term, like "darling."

kolam (koh-luhm): temporary household art, in which drawings are made on the floor with rice flour or rice paste.

kunju (koon-joo): animal or bird baby.

kutti (koot-tee): little, as in "little one"; used affectionately.

kuyil (koo-yil): songbird belonging to the cuckoo family. The male is black with red eyes, the female speckled. The song of the kuyil is said to foretell the coming of the rains.

Mahishasuramardhini (muh-hee-shah-soo-ruh-muhr-<u>thee</u>-nee): long composite name for the goddess, meaning "killer of the *asura*, or demon, Mahisha."

mami (mah-mee): literally, Mother's brother's wife, but generally used, especially by children, to refer to any older female.

Maya, Mahamaya (mah-yah, muh-hah-mah-yah): names of the goddess who put the tyrant Kamsa's armies to sleep and saved the infant god Krishna.

murukku (moo-rook-koo): crunchy snack food made with rice paste and spices.

namaskaram (nuh-muhs-kah-ruhm): common greeting among Hindus, palms joined and raised to just in front of the face, head quickly bowed.

oonjal (oon-juhl): swing, like the large wooden swings in many houses in Chennai, capable of seating several people and hung from the ceiling of a house or porch by large wrought-iron chains.

paapa (pah-pah): child or young one.

paavum (pah-voom): poor thing.

payasam (pah-yuh-suhm): a milk sweet made most often with rice or noodles thinner than angel-hair pasta, spiced with cardamom or saffron, sometimes garnished with nuts.

ponnu (pon-noo): girl.

raja (rah-jah): king.

rajakumari (rah-juh-koo-mah-ree): princess.

Rama (rah-muh), also referred to respectfully as Ramar (Rah-muhr): an incarnation of the god Vishnu. Rama fought a war to free his beautiful wife, Sita, whom the demon Ravana had kidnapped.

rasam (ruh-suhm): dish flavored with sour tamarind, garnished with mustard seeds and chopped coriander, and eaten with rice.

salwar (suhl-vahr): loose cuffed pants worn with a kameez on top. A northern Indian dress now common everywhere in India.

sambar (sahm-bahr): spicy lentil dish with vegetables, flavored with tamarind and usually eaten with rice.

sathyam (suhth-yuhm): truth.

Sita (see-thah): Rama's wife, subject of many songs and poems.

sojji (sohj-jee): farina or Cream of Wheat, used to make halwa.

Tamil (thah-mizh): language spoken in the state of Tamil Nadu. The last letter of the word Tamil (phonetically written as *zh*) is actually a sound unique to this language, and not found in English at all. Some people pronounce it like the *le* in *whale*, some like the *r* in *roll*.

thatha (thah-thah): grandfather.

thayiru (thuh-yee-roo): yogurt, usually made at home with scalded milk and culture from a previous batch.

vellaikkara (vel-lie-kah-rah): white people, generally used for all people of European descent.

yenna (yen-nuh): what.